Solid Proof

Wendy Cartmell

Costa Press

Copyright © Wendy Cartmell 2016
Published by Costa Press
ISBN-13 978-1522985570
ISBN-10: 1522985573
Wendy Cartmell has asserted her right under the Copyright Designs and Patents Act 1998 to be identified as the author of this work.
All characters and events in this publication, other than those in the public domain, are fictitious and any resemblance to real persons, living or dead is purely coincidental
This is a work of fiction and not meant to represent faithfully military, or police, policies and procedures. All and any mistakes in this regard are my own.
Inspired by a friend and fellow writer.

Praise for Wendy Cartmell

'A pretty extraordinary talent' –
Best Selling Crime Thrillers
'This is genre fiction at its best, suspense that rivets and a mystery that keeps you guessing.' –
A R Symmonds on Goodreads.

Also by Wendy Cartmell

Sgt Major Crane books:

Steps to Heaven
40 Days 40 Nights
Honour Bound
Cordon of Lies
Regenerate
Hijack
Glass Cutter
Solid Proof

Emma Harrison Mysteries

Past Judgement
Mortal Judgement

One

There it was, Crane's only clue. A single shoe on the garage floor. The crime scene lights picked it out as though it were placed there as part of a fashion magazine photo shoot. The crime scene photographer adding to that illusion, as he walked around the inanimate object photographing it from all angles, although he was dressed in a white paper suit with a mask over his face, instead of some trendy 'I've just thrown this together' attire.

Crane walked around the red glossy stiletto himself when the forensic photographer had finished. But it stubbornly remained what it was. Just a shoe. It told him precisely nothing. In all honesty Crane felt a bit of a fool, examining a shoe as though it were a body. Still, life was full of new experiences, especially in his job. But without doubt, this had to be one of the strangest encounters he'd ever had.

Crane looked again at the photograph that he was holding, depicting the owner of the said shoe. Her legs were long and slender, pushed straight by a pair of stiletto heels. A skirt swung around her knees and was teamed with a stylish, silk blouse. Her hair framed her face, neither short nor long, but teased artfully by an expensive hairdresser. The kind of hairstyle that looked natural, but was probably anything but.

"Well?" asked DI Anderson.

"Well what?" said Crane.

"Any thoughts?"

Crane caught sight of the DI's face and returned the grin. DI Derek Anderson of Aldershot Police and Sgt Major Tom Crane of the Special Investigation Branch of the Military Police knew each other well and Crane was keenly aware that Derek was trying to wind him up.

"Seriously, Derek, is this all we've got?" Crane asked, nodding towards the shoe.

"I'm afraid so," Derek consulted his notes. "It belongs to Janey Cunningham, a model who works under the name of Janey Carlton. Wife of one Major Cunningham, she seems to have disappeared into thin air."

Crane had to shake away the image of a genie disappearing with a puff of smoke back into the oil lamp he lived in.

"The couple had a meal at a restaurant in Farnham last night," Anderson was saying. "Upon arriving home, the Major realised he'd left his wallet in the restaurant. He dropped his wife off and immediately returned to Farnham to collect it. When he arrived back home that shoe was all that was left of Janey Cunningham. Her car is here and her clothes. The only thing missing, apart from her, is her handbag."

Anderson stuffed his notebook and his hands into his rumpled suit jacket pockets, seemingly oblivious to his grey wispy hair flying around in the wind, exposing the bald patch on his head.

"Has the Major tried to find her?" Subconsciously

Crane rubbed his hand over his own short, dark, curly hair, but it hadn't moved. It never did.

"He called her friends last night, waking some of them up, but everyone denied knowledge of her whereabouts. He phoned her mother, but she hadn't heard from her either. Janey's mobile phone was, and still is, turned off."

"No sign of a struggle?"

"Nope."

"So after that he called the police?"

"Not exactly," said Derek.

Crane raised an eyebrow.

"He waited until he woke up this morning and found she was still missing," Anderson continued. "When I was dispatched to the scene and heard that the call had come from an army officer, I phoned you."

"Why did the Major wait until this morning to ring the police?"

"That's what I hope we're about to find out," said Derek and led the way to the house.

The large detached house situated between Farnham and Aldershot had a separate two car garage and they walked from there, crunching over the gravelled drive, to the Major's home. A large, symmetrical, double fronted Georgian house awaited them, making Crane whistle.

"Maybe I should take a commission to officer rank, if this is what you can afford on a Major's pay," he said, taking in the imposing building, looking as though it were straight out of an article in the magazine Country Life.

"Family money," said Anderson.

"Eh?" Crane stopped walking and turned towards Anderson.

"Major Cunningham is a minor aristocrat, which means he's a major pain in the arse."

"Ah," said Crane nodding, deciding that the Major was probably one of those men playing at being soldiers, while they waited for papa to die, so they could take over the reins of the family estate. A prejudiced view, he knew, but he'd come across that type of officer before and as a result it coloured his judgement. "She's a model, you said?" Crane started walking again.

"Mmm. Works under her maiden name of Janey Carlton. I've never heard of her, but Mrs Derek has. Wants me to get her autograph when we find her," Derek delivered the line in his best, dry humoured voice and Crane had to struggle not to laugh out loud as Anderson pushed open the door to the house.

They stood in a large hallway on a black and white tiled floor. White closed doors led to various downstairs rooms and an imposing staircase swept onwards to the upper floor. At the sound of their feet, a door on their right opened and a uniformed policeman poked his head out.

"Ah, sir, Major Cunningham is here in the morning room, waiting for you," he told Anderson and flashing his eyes wide, opened the door, so they could walk through into the room.

Two

"The morning room, eh?" Crane couldn't resist the dig.

"I beg your pardon?" a man standing before an unlit fireplace with huge marble surround turned at Crane's words. He was dressed in casual clothes so crisp they had obviously been professionally cleaned. Crane mused that the creases in the Major's trousers were so severe the man was in danger of cutting his legs to ribbons. He wasn't in uniform, but quite honestly may as well have been, the twill trousers, muted shirt and tie covered by a V-necked pullover, were all in colours reminiscent of army fatigues.

"It's just that I've never been in one before, a morning room that is," Crane said, looking around the high-ceilinged majestic room which was filled with what appeared to be antique furniture. Crane fancied it was real, not reproduction, but to be honest he couldn't have told the difference between the two.

"And who might you be?"

"Me? Sgt Major Crane, SIB. And who might you be?" asked Crane, knowing full well who the man was.

"Major Cunningham. Why are you here, Crane?" Cunningham snapped. "I'd have thought this would be a civilian police matter."

"Oh dear, no," Crane replied watching the Major closely, feeling the distaste for the Branch that the man was radiating like an icy fog. But Crane had been there, done that and bought the t-shirt. Some officers, such as the one stood before him, hated the fact that SIB investigators on an active case, could interview who they wanted, when they wanted and where they wanted. It was one in the eye for the rank system that tried its best to keep those of a lower rank separated from those who were higher-ranking, such as sergeants or officers. Such men were a challenge that Crane just couldn't resist. "I'd be failing in my duty as a military investigator if I didn't assist DI Anderson here."

"Absolutely," Anderson agreed. "We're a team, Sgt Major Crane and I. Take us or leave us. But I'd advise co-operation if I were you, sir. If you want your wife back, that is."

"Of course I want my bloody wife back. Isn't that obvious?"

"Not immediately, sir, no," Crane chipped in.

"How dare you!" Cunningham roared, causing Crane to take a step backward in surprise and Anderson to step bodily between the two men.

"Please, Major, sit down. And you, as well, Crane." Once both men had complied, Anderson said, "I think Crane here is alluding to the fact that you didn't report Mrs Cunningham missing last night. Why was that, Major?"

Cunningham, sitting on the edge of a floral patterned settee, his elbows on his knees, looked down at the floor and said, "I thought she'd flounced off. She sometimes does that if we've had words."

"Words?"

Cunningham looked up at Anderson. "A few words, Inspector. A bit of an argument. Nothing much really. When I couldn't reach her last night, I figured she come home in the morning."

"But she hasn't."

"No."

"And what were those words about?" Crane asked.

The Major glared at Crane, then his whole body sagging said, "I'd said the wrong thing. It was something stupid about the fact that she was looking good for her age. But it touched a nerve. She didn't like being reminded that she was getting older. She'd been a bit touchy most of the evening, as though she was just waiting for me to say something wrong, which I, of course, unwittingly did."

"She hasn't been seen or heard of by her friends and family?"

The Major shook his head. "No. No one's heard from her at all."

Crane sat back and appraised the man in front of him, while Anderson continued with the questioning. Mid 40's, he guessed. Good looking, good teeth, good job, good background. A bit of a catch, he supposed, on the surface at any rate. But who knew what went on behind the façade of a golden couple. Was he moody, abusive, or cruel? Was she neurotic, spent all his money and was only interested in her career? He'd seen her picture in Tina's magazines, promoting some expensive product or other. Hair, make-up, clothes, it was all the same to Crane. She reminded him of Twiggy or Lulu, but 20 years younger than them, Janey Carlton being in her mid-40s, not mid-60s. But she was definitely out of that mould.

Crane tuned back in as Anderson was asking

Cunningham if the restaurant would confirm his story about leaving the wallet there last night.

"Of course they will. We're regular customers. They know me well."

Crane didn't know the restaurant in question, but knew that any restaurant in Farnham wasn't cheap. It was an affluent area with upmarket shops and eateries. A charming, old town with cobbled streets, wooden beamed houses and shops, complete with the obligatory fast train to London. Perfect, expensive, commuter territory.

"Well, thank you for your time, Major Cunningham," Anderson said as he stood up. "We'll be in touch."

"Is that it?"

"For now, yes," Crane said, deliberately leaving out the normal 'sir' he would be expected to utter to a senior officer.

"Well, what the hell are you going to do now? You can't just leave!" the Major jumped up as Crane and Anderson walked towards the door, his face suffusing with colour in his anger.

"We have to leave and get on with the business of trying to find your wife, sir," said Anderson. "Sitting here with you won't do anyone any good. If Mrs Cunningham gets in touch, or anyone else does with any news of her, tell the constable here," Anderson indicated the policeman who'd let them into the room and was still standing silently by the door. "He'll call the information in straight away. I've got the list of contact details of your friends and family," Anderson patted his pocket, "which is all I need for now."

With Major Cunningham still blustering, protesting at their leaving, they walked out.

Three

...It was always the bloody same. No matter what children's home, orphanage, or whatever the hell you wanted to call the places he'd been sent to, they were all as bad as each other. Always full of staff that didn't give a shit, kids that didn't give a shit and social workers that were so liberal and laid back they were practically flat on their backs. In most cases they were more interested in reading The Guardian than tackling the case files piling up on their desks. He had been in the system all his life. Weak at birth and with complicated health problems, no one had wanted to adopt him. Foster parents quickly tired of his anger and troublemaking, eventually succumbing to his indifference towards them and his determination to push anyone and everyone away, and sent him back. Back to the places he was desperate to get away from, but unable to work out how to.

As he was sent from one orphanage to another, they blurred into sameness. Same paint peeling, concrete cracked walls. Same smells of damp and boiled cabbage. Same rickety beds. Same lack of privacy. Same idiots in charge who were more interested in chatting over cups of tea, than doing any work.

His problem, of course, was that he was livid. It coloured his thinking, his judgment and his relationships. He was mad at his birth mother for fucking off, fuming at the gangs of bullies who picked on him and irate that he didn't have a family like 99% of the population seemed to have. As a result of the anger that was building inside him like storm clouds, most people gave him a wide berth. Lonely and isolated, he'd quickly realised that you couldn't rely on anyone. Only yourself.

His asthma, skin conditions and bad stomach started to clear up as he reached puberty and signalled a turning point in his miserable life. He was aware that he needed to bulk up. His thin and bony limbs not only looked pathetic but were ineffective when it came to running away from bullies trying to catch him, or throwing punches if he was surprised and cornered. He began to grab food wherever and whenever he could, ate as much as possible at meals and hid snacks in secret places around the grounds of whatever institution was his current home.

Under cover of darkness he started to exercise. Running helped his stamina. Shadow boxing made his reactions quicker. Push ups, pull ups and sit ups built muscle. As he grew, so did his reputation. Not only was he angry, he was now dangerous and the other kids quickly realised it was bad for their health to pick on him.

As his body matured, the additional oxygen coursing through his body, fed his brain. The water he drank whilst exercising helped with thinking and the food he ate at breakfast, that he'd once shunned, increased his ability to concentrate.

The teachers at school slowly began to notice the change in him. Most ignored it, as they did most of their pupils, preferring to take the easy route of teaching everyone the same thing, whether they understood it or not, or even already knew it. They couldn't care less about pushing the brighter children, nor giving those struggling extra help. But there were a couple that were different. The english teacher, a matronly looking woman, yet with an imperial air about her, began to lend him new and interesting books to read and then casually discussing them with him once they had been read. The mathematics teacher, a young, sharp minded, angle bodied, bony male, delighted him by opening up the world of computers and programming. Once hooked, he quickly became passionate about bits, bytes, binary code and operating systems.

And then came the turning point, the pivotal birthday. When he turned 18, he was turfed out of the latest local authority home, given a housing association flat and told to get on with it. He was officially an adult and no one else's responsibility but his own. Weaker orphans fell apart at this point. Having spent a lifetime cossetted from decision making, money management, cooking and employment, turned adrift on the sea of adulthood, they floundered. But not him. Here was the release he'd been waiting for all his life. Thanking those two disparate but equally effective teachers, he left school, moved into his flat and arranged for the fastest internet connection he could get. He then stole a laptop from an unsuspecting traveller who was waiting for his train at the local railway station.

He was finally on his way.

Four

"Jessica, Grace, breakfast!"

Tyler Wells watched his wife moving around the kitchen of their London house, multi-tasking as she made coffee, laid the table, buttered toast and sprinkled cereal out of battered boxes. A small, lithe, honey blond, she moved with the ease and grace of a dancer.

"Girls! I said breakfast!" she called through the kitchen door and was rewarded by the sight and sound of two blond-haired girls banging down the stairs and trying to get through the doorway at the same time.

"Hey," said Jessica, "Stop pushing me!"

"I'm not," said Grace, squeezing through the door first, "You're in my way. And anyway I should go through first, I'm the eldest."

The girls were, as usual, dressed alike and not just because of the school uniform of grey skirt and green polo tops and blazers. Their hair was platted and hung down their respective backs and both wore identical glasses and shoes. As Grace had just said, she was the eldest by 5 minutes. The twins, his wife and their house, were Tyler's world.

As the girls shovelled cereal into their mouths, Tyler

extended and then bent his arm as he checked the time on his Rolex wristwatch.

"Right everyone, time I was off. Be good," he kissed each girl's head, "and you too," he smiled into his wife's eyes, tucking a lock of her hair behind her ear. Penny returned the smile and pecked him on the cheek. Tyler grabbed his briefcase and opening the door, stepped out into the crisp morning air.

As he strode along the quiet London street, away from the very expensive Victorian terraced house that was his home, he reflected on how lucky he was to have the life he had, particularly after such a bad start. He was told that his mother had given him up for adoption at birth, presumably unable to cope with a baby at an early age. It seemed that single act of selflessness (or some might think of it as an act of selfishness) was what had given him such a good start in life. The middle class couple, who had taken him in, loved him as if he had been their own biological son. Perhaps more so, as they'd been desperate to adopt a child after they'd found that Mrs Wells was unable to conceive.

Tyler had always known he was adopted, but because of his adoptive parent's love and support, had come to think of it as a privilege. As a result he hadn't felt any need to search for the woman who had rejected him at birth. She had never been in his life and he hoped it would stay that way. He preferred to look forward and not hanker after the past.

In the nurturing environment of his adopted life, he had been able to develop to his full capabilities and was now a hedge-fund manager in a large London firm. Despite the public outrage at the banker's bonuses and disgust at the way the financial sector had caused the economic recession, Tyler had kept his job and his bonuses and was therefore able to amply provide for his family.

His strides in his all leather brogues had by now taken him to the tube station and he joined the flow of commuters as they made their way into central London. They followed each other like lemmings down into the bowels of the underground, where tube trains gobbled them up and then rattled and rolled their way through the network of tunnels. The carriages disgorged their passengers at each stop, before wolfing up more, to keep the belly of the beast filled to capacity.

Tyler looked around at his fellow travellers as he dangled perilously from a strap attached to the ceiling of the rocking and rolling carriage. Men and women, old and young, of all skin colours, surrounded him. Each kept their own counsel. No one chatted. Several were reading, even more fiddling with their mobile phones. But no one interacted with each other. He felt a slight prickle on the back of his neck, as though someone behind him was paying him rather too much attention. Turning around, he scanned the people nearest to him. No one was paying him any mind. Immediately around him was a young, suited woman, who was reading. An older man looked world weary as he stared unseeing out of a window. A gaggle of school girls giggled amongst themselves, dressed in distinctive brown and yellow uniforms. Finally a man, sitting nearby, was casually dressed and hunched over his mobile, his face hidden by a baseball cap.

Tyler turned back and gripped his briefcase handle tightly, in readiness of disembarking, as the train juddered, brakes screaming, into his station. But once again that strange feeling haunted him and a shiver went down his back. His scalp began to itch underneath his wild dark hair that he always seemed unable to tame and his dark eyes narrowed. But not being able to turn back around, because of the crush of people pushing forwards towards the door, he had no option but to stand there, under the scrutiny of the unknown person, until he was released from the carriage and he and his fellow passengers spilled out onto the platform.

Deciding he was being irrational, he followed his fellow lemmings up the escalators and out onto the bright street. As he strode along, Tyler felt himself changing as he took the short walk from the underground station to his office. Gone now was the rush of emotion he had felt for his family. Gone now was the musing over their antics. Gone was the disquiet he had felt in the train. As though pulling a cloak over his family persona, the business side of his character rose to the fore. By the time he walked through the glass doors into his office building, he had morphed into the hard-nosed hedge fund dealer that he was. Dressed in a pin-striped suit, crisp white shirt and colourful silk tie, he was a driven, focused business man, oblivious to those around him, eager to get to his desk and start his day.

Five

As Crane and Anderson walked back to their cars, back towards the garage with the lone shoe and crime scene techs crawling all over the structure, they pondered the conundrum of Janey Cunningham's vanishing trick.

"Well?" asked Derek. "What do you think?"

"Of her disappearance? Or of the Major?"

"Her disappearance. I'm well aware what you think of the Major that was evident."

"Yes, well," Crane lit a cigarette to draw a line under that particular part of the conversation. "It's bloody interesting," was his take on their problem. He began wandering up and down in front of his car. "I could really do with a whiteboard, but as we're stood on the drive of a large house, any chance you could make notes, Derek?"

"Oh, God, here we go," said Anderson, well used to Crane's brainstorming and obligingly scrabbled in his pocket for his notebook and pen.

"Right," Crane still hadn't stopped pacing. "Let's imagine the possible scenarios. First, the Major killed his wife on the way home after dinner at the restaurant, dumped her body somewhere, went home, left the shoe in the garage and then returned to the restaurant to give himself an alibi."

Anderson nodded. "Good one."

"Or," Crane continued, "He killed her at home, left her shoe in the garage, went back to the restaurant and dumped her body on the way."

"Fair enough," said Anderson, chewing the end of his pen. "What if it wasn't him?"

Crane took a few drags of his cigarette and then said. "In that case, someone was in the process of burgling the property. She disturbed him. He killed her and took the body with him, not knowing a shoe had dropped off her foot."

Anderson looked up from his notebook. "In that case, we'd better get forensics into the house. That will help with that theory. My turn now. How about someone had a grudge or something against her, had been stalking her and seeing a window of opportunity when the Major went back to the restaurant, killed her and took the body with him."

"Nice one," said Crane, throwing his cigarette away. "Anything else?"

"Yep. How about she's been kidnapped? They look pretty well off. We might get a ransom demand."

Crane contemplated that theory, leaning back against his car and putting his hands in his black coat pocket that he wore over his dark work suit, white shirt and regimental tie. "Maybe we're looking at this the wrong way," he said.

"Oh yes?" Anderson asked after finishing scribbling down the previous theory.

"Yes. Maybe she's just left him. She saw her window of opportunity, as you so aptly described it and so just ran. I know there are no clothes missing, but her handbag is. What about her passport?"

Anderson flicked back in his notebook. "I asked the Major that question when I first arrived. Oh here it is," and Anderson peered at the page. "Yes, it's missing as far as he can tell. At least it's not in its usual place."

"So she could have done a moonlight flit."

"A what?"

"Sorry, Derek, it's an expression that means she ran away in the middle of the night, leaving everything behind. People used to do that when they owed money and they couldn't pay it back. They just ran away in the middle of the night, hence 'moonlight flit'."

"Very interesting I'm sure, but how does it help us? Why would she have done a - whatever you called it?"

Crane referred back to his earlier thoughts. "We don't know what went on behind those closed doors," he indicated the imposing double doors of the house behind them. "The Major says they are happy, they certainly from the outside look like a golden couple. But are they really? She could have been a right bitch, him a big bully. Despite all the trappings of wealth they could have money problems."

"I see what you mean. So we need to poke into their backgrounds, their marriage, their families and friends. Let's find out what they are really like, behind that public image." Anderson delved into his pocket and picked out a piece of paper. "I've got details of their friends and families here. Let's see what we can find out, we've too many questions and it's about time we got some answers. Shall we take my car?"

Six

...Half an hour earlier, the man had watched Tyler Wells leave his house. But he had not moved from his position in a car a short way down the road. He had his mobile phone in his hand, as though checking his emails or text messages, but his real focus was the house, not the piece of moulded plastic in his hand. He smiled as he caught sight of Penny Wells and the two girls spill out of the house and begin their walk to the local school. Because she normally went for a run after depositing the girls at school, Penny was dressed in a designer track suit and the observer had timed her absence several times over the past weeks and knew he had around 30 minutes before she returned.

Once the family turned the corner at the bottom of the street he then climbed out of the car and sauntered over to the Wells' house. He had on dark, nondescript clothes. A baseball cap and a hoodie obscured his features from nosey neighbours. Arriving at the house he got down on one knee as though to tie his lace, but in reality picked the lock and opened the now unresisting door. Closing it behind him, he stood in the hall taking in the atmosphere of the house. He breathed deeply and inhaled the aroma of freshly washed hair and clothes, tinged with a lingering smell of slightly burnt toasted bread. So this is what family life smells like, he thought.

Somewhere in the annals of his memory, something stirred. One of his foster homes had been similar to this; a warm, welcoming, messy, yet happy house. But the parents already had two children of their own, youngsters who hated the interloper. After being frequently bullied, pinched, punched and locked in rooms, he finally retaliated, punching and knocking out the younger boy; which necessitated in a trip to hospital for his victim and a trip back to the children's home for him. The memory hardened his resolve. He would never be accepted anywhere, by anyone. He was alone and it was all the fault of his birth mother. Feeling the sting of rejection once more and the anger which clenched his fists and jaw, he continued with his mission.

Ignoring the kitchen and downstairs rooms, he walked silently upstairs and found Tyler and Penny's bedroom. The bed was still rumpled, unmade since Tyler and Penny had left it. He poked his head in the en-suite bathroom and saw yesterday's clothes were discarded on the floor. Damp towels were flung over the top of the shower stall and Penny's make up and creams were jumbled next to the sink.

Returning to the bedroom, he opened the wardrobe and reached in and pulled out a handful of Penny's clothes. Pulling them towards him, he buried his face in them, the particular smell of her filling his nostrils. It was obvious she favoured Chanel No 5 as her perfume of choice. But he felt no emotion. No stirring, no longing, no jealousy. She was merely a tool in his quest for revenge. After pushing the clothes back into the wardrobe and closing the doors, he turned his attention to the chest of drawers. After several unsuccessful attempts, he found the one he wanted - the drawer filled with Penny's underwear. Rooting through the bras and knickers he picked out a particularly sexy matching set of ivory lace covered bra and barely-there thong. He made the bed and then laid the set of lingerie carefully on the now smooth duvet cover, placing the bra above the thongs. An invitation if ever there was one.

Checking his watch, the interloper turned and made his way out of the house, closing the door behind him. Pleased with his work, he decided he would leave his mark on the downstairs of the house the next time he visited.

Seven

To Crane's shock, the car stopped outside a local authority property in Ash, a small village situated between Aldershot and Guildford. "You're kidding me," he said to Anderson. "Have we come to the right place?"

Anderson consulted his notes and nodded his confirmation. "Mrs Cunningham's parents live here, at number 30," and he indicated a semi-detached property in the middle of the row of houses they were parked opposite. "Goes by the name of Carlton, Janey's maiden name."

Crane saw that all the properties were solid semi-detached houses. Grey pebbledash adorned the top half of the walls, matching the grey sky of the morning. The whole area seemed washed with grey, more urban sprawl and less pretty English chocolate box village. "From rags to riches," he muttered under his breath, as he clambered out of the car.

By the time Crane joined him, Derek had already knocked on the door, which had been opened by an elderly woman, who looked more bird than person. Her head bobbed and nodded when Anderson asked if her daughter was Janey Cunningham and her hands fluttered from her grey hair, to her apron and back again.

Anderson introduced them and after he explained that they were there because they were having difficulty locating Janey, they were led into a surprisingly large lounge, or at least it would have been if it had been empty. As it was, it was filled to the brim with furniture. Glass fronted cabinets contained china dolls, figurines and clowns. Footstools joined various coffee tables dotted around the floor. Crane couldn't help notice a huge TV and stereo system which was squeezed in along one wall. The room was decorated with large flower printed wallpaper, again giving the illusion that the room was smaller than it actually was. They sat down at Mrs Carlton's invitation and after refusing a cup of tea, Anderson asked for some background on her daughter.

"Janey was always such a good girl," Mrs Carlton said. "Tried hard at school and stuff, was always popular and had lots of friends."

"How did she become a model?" Crane wanted to know.

"Oh, she was spotted," Mrs Carlton sat straighter on her chair. "Ever so exciting it was," she smiled at the memory. "Janey was walking around the shops in Guildford one Saturday morning with her friends and she was stopped by a man who said he was a spotter from a modelling agency. He gave her his card and asked her to ring him. Said they were looking for someone just like her."

"I take it she rang him?"

"Oh yes, Mr Anderson. Her dad wasn't keen mind you. Caused ructions it did. He said it was a bad business to be in, full of drugs and such and that she didn't know what she was getting into. She was at college at the time and he wanted her to finish her studies."

"What was she studying?"

"Beauty therapy and stuff, you know. She was always interested in clothes and make-up."

Janey Cunningham wasn't much of an academic then, Crane thought to himself. It figured.

"So what happened?" Anderson prompted Mrs Carlton, whose eyes had wandered away from them and she seemed lost in thought.

"Oh, well, her dad said she wasn't to go to London to see the modelling agency, but I gave her the money to go. I couldn't go with her myself, as her dad would have smelled a rat, so she went with a friend. By the time her dad found out, she'd been taken on by the agency and had her first booking. When he realised how much she was being paid, well he changed his tune after that."

"Where is Mr Carlton? Is he at work?" Crane asked.

"Oh, he died a few years back now," she said smiling, making Crane wonder what Mrs Carlton had thought of her husband. He would normally have mumbled something about offering his condolences, but in the light of her happy face he swallowed his words instead.

Mrs Carlton walked over to a long cabinet placed under the window. On the top of it were row upon row of photos of Janey. She picked one and handed it to Anderson.

"This is from that first job," she said and after glancing at it, Anderson passed it to Crane.

It showed a girl of about 16 or 17, fresh faced and

innocent, looking slightly bewildered if anything. It was a far cry from the studied poses of Janey's later work, which radiated sensuality. Crane wondered if the change in her was for the better. Comparing it with the photo in his pocket, he preferred the younger girl to the cold shrewd professional she seemed to have become. Was it a natural progression as she became older, or something more calculating? He didn't know, but the change didn't endear her to Crane.

"Mrs Carlton," Anderson said gently. "When did you last hear from your daughter?"

"Oh, let me see," she said, her hands plucking at her apron. "It must have been a couple of weeks ago, maybe a month. She rings when she can, but she's so busy, you know, what with work and the Major and that."

"Yes, of course," Anderson agreed.

Crane saw the older woman's eyes begin to water and her hand start to shake. "You don't think anything's happened to her, do you?" She implored, rather than asked, obviously hoping they'd say there was nothing at all wrong.

"At the moment, we don't know," said Anderson. "It's just that she hasn't been seen since last night and she's not answering her mobile phone. At the moment our enquiries are more of a precaution than anything."

Crane heard the kind words Anderson was saying to Janey's mother, but both of them knew the odds were that there was something wrong. For surely if Janey Cunningham had wanted to leave her husband, she would have made sure he left the house, not her. She seemed the type that would make the best of any situation and be determined to turn the tables in her favour. Crane couldn't get the coldness reflected in her eyes as she posed for the camera out of his mind.

With promises to call Mrs Carlton if there was any news, they left her to her photos and memories and struck out for Aldershot Garrison, to interview Major Cunningham's Commanding Officer.

Eight

…Well aware he needed to earn a living, but shunning the world of commerce, and people come to that, he put the stolen laptop to good use. All sorts of distance learning programmes could be accessed via the internet and access them he did. His voracious quest for information honed his skills and bolstered his coffers, as hacking turned out to be a most lucrative pastime. He started cautiously at first, before graduating to stealing information to order, for a price. He would never forget the thrill of that first payday. The first money he'd earned, maybe not by legal means, but he'd earned it all the same. And it sure beat working on the tills at his local supermarket, which was where most of the idiots from the children's home ended up. £10 an hour wasn't his goal in life, more like £10 a minute or even £10 a second.

As he climbed up the pecking order of the darker side of the on-line community, he learned what worked and what did not. What was viable and what wasn't. What request was too great a risk, no matter how high the price that was offered. He had no intention of going to prison, which were institutions not dissimilar to the children's homes he'd live in all his life. He valued his freedom, anonymity and money.

But always, burning like a cancer in his soul was his hatred for his mother. The bitch who had given birth to him and then run away from her responsibility. When he knew enough about virtual back doors, stealing passwords via keystroke loggers and other such tricks, he'd broken into the social service's computer system. It wasn't hard to find his records in the system, as someone had obligingly inputted the written records from the past 30 years into the central computer system, in the Government's bureaucratic quest for paperless offices in the 21st century.

His name was his real one. No one had seemed to see any need to change it. He hadn't been adopted and therefore taken his adoptive family name and no one had cared enough to protect his anonymity. As he obviously also knew his birth date, he put the two together and hell, it was like taking candy from a baby.

From the central records he found where he had been born and from there it was easy to hack into that system and get the address for his mother at the time of his birth. A house that was still occupied by his grandmother. An address that meant he now knew who, and more importantly, where his mother was. But the additional information he gleaned from those records startled him. He had a brother. A twin. A brother who had been adopted. A brother who had also left him. Between the two of them they'd isolated him, left him to rot, turned the key to his prison and walked away without a second glance.

They would both pay for that.

Nine

Crane knocked on Captain Draper's door. "Boss, got a minute? I've DI Anderson with me."

"Oh, Crane, it's you, yes, come in."

Anderson and Crane walked into Captain Draper's office, the current boss of the Military Police and SIB in Provost Barracks, Aldershot. A 22 year veteran of the army, Draper had taken a commission after achieving the rank of Warrant Officer Class 1, to ensure he stayed in the Regiment instead of taking the obligatory retirement for a non-commissioned officer. Should Crane ever reach that rank he wasn't yet sure what he'd do. The thought of leaving the army was too horrible for Crane to contemplate, but becoming an officer? Well the jury was still out on that one.

Draper stood to welcome Anderson and the two men shook hands over Draper's desk.

"We've just been to see Major Cunningham's CO," Crane said, "so thought we'd drop in and bring you up to date."

"Thanks, Crane. Good to see you, Derek," Draper said. "Bit of a strange case here, from what I understand."

"That's right," replied Anderson. "At the moment we're not sure that a crime has actually been committed. But, if there has and we weren't doing anything about it, given who she is and who his family is..." Anderson trailed off.

"Precisely," agreed Draper. Turning to Crane he asked, "Anything from Cunningham's CO?"

"Not really, sir, just the usual bollocks that he is a great soldier and leader of men."

"Maybe he is."

"You haven't met him," was Crane's swift retort, making Draper smile.

Draper was as unlike an officer as Crane had met. To be fair the men who were NCO's and had then taken a commission, were often more respected by the men under their command. The new boss having moved through the ranks had been responsible for numerous men under his command and spoke the same language as they did, as it were. It was therefore much easier to relate to him and he was also much more conducive to Crane's ideas than his previous boss, Captain James Edwards had been. The thought of that twit made Crane shudder. Not that it had all been plain sailing with Draper. He could act in the interests of the brass upstairs, rather than his men, for after all being an officer was far more of a political job than being an NCO. But Draper and Crane had seemed to strike a good balance. Draper seemingly appreciated Crane's need for individuality, which Draper then tempered with rules and regulations. But only when absolutely necessary, which was normally when Draper needed to get Crane off whatever hook he'd managed to spear himself on.

"So where are we now?"

"We're setting up downstairs," Crane said. "I want there to be lots of visibility for the enquiry, to keep any passing noses happy that we're doing our job."

Draper smiled sardonically.

"And then once we've handed out tasks, we'll be off on the road again to interview the Major's family."

"Right, off you go then," said Draper. Then hesitating he said, "Nice to see you, Derek, sorry I wasn't dismissing you, just Crane here."

"Don't worry, I'm used to your military ways these days, Crane here makes sure I get plenty of practice."

"Well, no offence meant."

"None taken," said Anderson and they left Draper to his paperwork, with a slight flush receding from his face.

After walking down a flight of stairs, Crane and Anderson pushed their way into the SIB office. It was a large open space, dotted with desks. A meeting area and Crane's office off to one side were afforded a bit of privacy by moveable screens. Crane made for a whiteboard that Sgt Billy Williams was sticking things onto.

"Oh good, you've started," said Crane.

"Yes, boss," said Billy. "I've just downloaded the photos that DI Anderson's office sent through. I'm doing a bit of a family tree for the Major."

"Excellent," said Crane and after shouting for someone to get them cups of tea, he and Anderson settled down for a briefing from Billy.

"Right. Here he is, Major Clive Cunningham. His family are rich and he's the first born son of Lord Garford with an estate in Garford nr Abingdon. He joined the army about 10 years ago as it seems he's not interested in the estate and learning how to run it for when his father dies. His younger brother Quentin runs the sprawl instead. So our friend Clive just reaps the rewards of the family money, spending it instead of working to increase it or protect it."

"What about Janey Cunningham?"

"Janey Cunningham works under her maiden name of Janey Carlton. From a far humbler background, she is, or was, a successful model."

"Yes we know that, we've just been to see her mother. What else can you tell us?" said Crane.

Billy went smoothly on, "She is an only child and relies heavily on a relationship with her best friend Laura Battle." Billy pointed to a picture of a carefully made up woman, which was obviously a publicity shot of some kind. "Laura Battle is her agent and confidant."

"So not someone she grew up with?"

"No, boss," said Billy. "Janey seems to have left her earlier life completely behind, like a snake sloughing off a skin. The only regular contact I could find out about was with her mother and I think that's sporadic at best."

"That's the impression we got too," said Anderson.

Billy continued, "As you know she's a model, but it seems she's getting less work as she gets older. However, she made her fortune modelling and is independently wealthy."

"Interesting," said Crane. "That begs the question - does he want her money? Do we think she's left him as he is violent? Abusive? Controlling? Somehow I can't believe they are the golden couple they project themselves to be. I think we need to dig deeper."

"I agree, Crane," said Anderson. "Laura Battle first, I think, followed by the Major's family," he said scraping back his chair and standing up.

Crane stood as well, but before they left he got Anderson to photocopy a page out of his notebook. Crane handed it to Billy. "Put these theories up on the board will you? When we get back we can start to work our way through them, we should have more information by then."

Ten

Tyler Wells groaned and stretched in his chair at the end of a long day. He glanced through his notes. Not bad, he mused. Taking everything into consideration he was just about up on the day. Which was okay. Not great, but okay. He was happy with the deals so far this month. The progress of his portfolios was slow and steady, which meant that when he pulled off a big deal, buying low before selling high, making money for himself as well as his clients, there would be no big dips to offset his earnings. Some of the younger men at the firm were risk takers; constantly making snap decisions, boasting about their highs and trying to bury the lows. They hadn't yet realised that with great dips that dragged down their overall totals, they would do better if they could curb their wilder side. Not to mention the burn-out. He'd seen too many of them leave the firm, dark circles under their eyes, with sallow skin and shaking hands, unable to take the pressure of even one more deal.

He stood and shrugged into his suit jacket, the silk lining whispering as it slid over his white shirt, which wasn't as crisp as it had been when he'd first arrived at work that morning. He was just checking over his desk, collecting his pen, keys and mobile, when the phone on his desk rang. Hesitating for a moment, he picked up the receiver, the call of work still strong, even though he was just about to leave.

"Wells," he barked into the receiver. No answer. "This is Tyler Wells," he said, his voice losing some of its harshness. "How can I help you?"

But there was still no reply. Tyler strained to listen for any sound on the other end of the line and fancied he could hear faint sounds of traffic; the creak and groan of lorry springs, the hiss of air brakes and then the distant hark of a horn, the wail cut off as the caller disconnected.

Tyler looked at the telephone receiver he still held in his hand as though it would tell him what the hell was going on. That wasn't the first such call he'd received that day. Someone had been calling on his direct line and then not speaking when he answered. There had been one such call that morning, one in the afternoon and again just then. He replaced the receiver hoping that was the end of it, but couldn't as easily dismiss the feeling of disquiet that was running its cold fingers across the back of his neck.

He grabbed his briefcase and walked across the open plan office to the lifts. He pushed the button to call one, grinding his teeth as he waited and checking his watch. 6pm. With any luck he'd be back home before the twins went to bed. They were looking forward to the next chapter in Alice through the Looking Glass. The extent of their vocabulary and their thirst for books never ceased to amaze him. He didn't know where they'd got it from. He wasn't a great reader, neither was his wife. It must be the influence of the private school they attended. The fees took quite a large chunk out of his salary but he and Penny had agreed that the girls' education came first. Besides, living near central London meant that more than one car wasn't necessary and so the money was better spent on the twins.

The elevator doors slid open and he slipped through them, turning in the small space to face the doors, staring out of them back towards his desk, as he waited for them to close. Just before they slid silently together, he heard the phone on his desk start to ring again, causing him to frown. What the hell was going on? Then the doors closed completely, cutting off the sound of the phone that echoed through the empty office and the lift whisked him away towards the ground floor and home.

Eleven

Laura Battle's offices were housed in a shed at her home near Reading. Well, not so much a shed, Crane had to concede, more a low slung suite of offices with a covering of overlapping cedar panels and banks of clear glass that looked onto a courtyard and what could best be described as a Japanese garden. There was a web of small pathways meandering through foliage and vegetation, which appealed to Crane's sense of order and purpose. Water tinkled from the fountain, or at least Crane thought it would have been tinkling, if the sound wasn't masked by the rain, which was pissing down. Their arrival had clearly been observed as a door opened and a woman appeared, watching Crane and Anderson from the doorway as they climbed out of the car and ran for the building.

Anderson thrust his warrant card in the woman's face and gasped, "Aldershot Police," shaking the rain off his coat as the woman let them in. "DI Anderson and Sgt Major Crane Royal Military Police," Anderson introduced them as Crane took stock of the woman standing in front of them.

Her skin was deeply lined and tanned, but with an

orange hue to it. Sun lover or sunbed lover, Crane wondered. Either way it wasn't a good look. Her hair was bouffant and seemed to have a life of its own as it framed the top of her head in no discernable style. She was stick-thin, dressed in a severe business suit and sucking on a cigarette. She said nothing.

"Ms Battle?" Crane enquired.

"Yes," she grudgingly said. "How can I help the police?"

"It's about your friend and client, Janey Carlton," Anderson said. "Could we ask you a few questions please? We're hoping you can help us with our enquiries as to her whereabouts."

Laura Battle seemed to consider their request before nodding. She turned on her heel and walked over to a group of settees. She sat almost sideways on the seat of one of them, knees together and indicated that they should join her.

"So, what's Janey done now?" she asked. Her voice was gravelly and low and her words were followed by a cough that had a worrying rattle deep in her chest.

"Nothing, as far as we're aware, it's just that she appears to be missing," said Anderson and went on to explain about the events of last night.

"Typical," Battled pronounced.

"Really? She does this sort of thing often?" asked Crane is disbelief as that wasn't the impression he and Anderson had got from her husband.

Battle took one last deep drag of her cigarette and then put it out in the ashtray, where it joined what looked like a whole packet's worth of butts. "Let's say she's inclined to the dramatic," said Battle.

"So you haven't seen her in the last, say 48 hours?"

Battle shook her head.

"How would you describe her?" asked Crane.

"Let's see, the professional Janey, or the personal Janey?" Battle seemed to consider her own question.

Both men kept quiet and, as expected, Laura Battle filled the silence.

"As far as work is concerned, she's the consummate professional. Takes most bookings that are offered, arrives on time, does a good job and makes the photographer and the client happy."

"And personally?" prompted Anderson.

"She's my best friend."

"That's not what I asked."

"No, I suppose not," Battle smiled, which cracked her pancake make-up and turned her lips into a garish grin. "Okay, she's self-absorbed, greedy, takes drugs. Smokes to keep her weight down, hardly eats and is anorexic."

"Oh," Anderson appeared startled. "That was honest at any rate."

Again that sardonic smile from Battle. As Crane studied her, she appeared to be enjoying herself, deliberately being provocative, proffering unexpected facts, showing a different side of Janey than Crane and Anderson had expected. She opened a small silver case on a nearby low table, extracted a cigarette and lit it with a lighter from her pocket. She didn't offer Anderson or Crane one and Crane resisted the temptation to take out his own packet. Tipping her head back, she blew a long stream of smoke towards the ceiling.

Crane said, "Does she have much work on at the moment?"

"No so much, no."

"Because?"

"Because of her age. It happens. I did warn her."

"How was she taking it, this slow down?"

Battle shrugged, "You know," she said.

"No we don't," said Anderson.

"Not particularly well." Battle settled back against the settee and crossed her legs. Anderson raised his eyebrows, questioningly. "Alright," Battle sighed. "She hated the fact her career was waning. Is that what you wanted to know?"

Crane leaned forwards, "Where do you think she is?"

"No idea," she said, but didn't hold Crane's gaze, her eyes sliding to the left to focus on a painting on the wall.

"Do you think this could be nothing more than a publicity stunt?" he asked.

"How would I know?" Battle said. But Crane thought she did know. He had a feeling she knew far more than she was prepared to admit for the moment.

"Very well, Ms Battle," said Anderson, standing. "Here's my card. Please let me know if you hear from her, or she turns up here."

Laura Battle stood as well. "Of course," she answered and took the proffered card.

But Crane decided he wouldn't hold his breath. Being contacted by Laura Battle would be the last thing he'd expect.

As the door to the offices closed behind them Crane looked up. The sky was clearing, the rain gone, leaving gleaming, and glistening rain drops decorating the plants in the Japanese garden. But it didn't have a calming effect on Crane. The whole place seemed wrong to him somehow. It was too posed and too cold - just like its owner.

As Anderson drove away, Crane said, "I think she's hiding something from us."

"Do you think this is a publicity stunt then?" Anderson asked.

"I'm not sure. In fact I'm not sure about any of them."

"I fancy her husband," Anderson said.

"Oh please, Derek," Crane laughed.

Anderson flushed at the faux pa and said, "You know what I mean, I fancy that her husband has something to do with her disappearance."

"You think he's killed her?"

Anderson nodded his agreement.

"Well," said Crane, "That's not going to stick without a body and some forensic evidence and at the moment we've neither. Still, onward and upward, let's go and see Major Cunningham's brother at the family estate."

Twelve

It wasn't too long a trek from Reading, in the direction of Abingdon. The satnav interrupted their conversation every now and again with its robotic sounding directions. They stopped at the gates of the estate. They were tall and imposing, at least 8 feet high and a wall ran from each side of them, running away into the distance. But the gates were open, so they drove on, towards a mansion that could be seen peeping through trees some way away.

The drive wound its way through a wooded area and at one point Crane fancied he spotted a deer bounding away as it was startled by their car. They pulled up in front of an old house, not quite of Downton Abbey's size, but beautiful in its proportions and built of old creamy red brick. As they parked the car, a man walked up to them. Crane and Anderson held up their identification and asked to speak to someone from the family, preferably Lord Garford.

"I'm afraid you'll have to make do with me," the man said. "I'm Quentin Cunningham," and he held out his hand.

As Crane took it, feeling a short firm handshake

under his fingers, he asked, "Clive Cunningham's brother?"

"That's me, how can I help?"

Anderson explained that Janey Cunningham was missing and they were making enquiries as to her possible whereabouts.

"Well, she's not here," Quentin said. "Here is probably the last place she'd be. Look, walk with me, would you? We'll go to the estate office."

They followed Cunningham around the side of the house, past a kitchen garden and onward towards a stable block. Several stalls were in use, their owner's looking out at them, snorting and shaking their heads, their manes flicking and ears twitching. Crane found their stares disconcerting and was glad when they left the horses behind and walked into an office.

"Cuppa?" Quentin asked, indicating a kettle and a tray of assorted mugs.

"No, you're alright, thanks," said Anderson. "We don't want to take up too much of your time."

Quentin invited them to sit down and Crane and Anderson managed to find a couple of straight backed wooden chairs that were free of newspapers. There was a large corkboard along one wall with rosettes and pictures pinned to it, along with newspaper clippings.

Quentin saw Crane looking at the board and said, "We do pretty well with the horses."

"Racing?"

Quentin nodded. "Not top level stuff, nothing like the stables from Lambourn, but we do well enough, it pays for the horses' keep. I enjoy it and so do they," he nodded in the direction of the stables.

Anderson explained to Quentin that Janey Cunningham hadn't been seen since last night and that they were doing a bit of background digging, talking to family members and her colleagues, to try and find out what might have happened to her.

"Do you know her well?" Crane asked when Anderson had finished.

"I know of her, rather than know her," Quentin said. "They don't come here much and when they do she swans around being all aloof and above us, constantly checking her appearance and lipstick. It drives me nuts all that posturing and posing."

Crane could understand that. Quentin was dressed in jodhpurs and an old jumper with leather elbow patches which had bits of straw poking out of it. Not exactly haute-couture. "So your brother doesn't take much interest in the estate then? If he doesn't come here much…"

"No, hates it all. The house, the estate, the parents. Couldn't wait to get away."

"Hence the army?"

Quentin nodded. "He won't be back here much until father dies, then it'll be a different story."

"Why?" Anderson looked puzzled.

But Crane thought he knew what Quentin was talking about. "He's the elder brother," Crane said.

"Exactly. He inherits the lot, the estate the money..." Quentin's voice trailed away.

Crane should have felt vilified, after all his suspicions about the Major were correct, playing into his theory about him being the type of officer he hated, but instead he found himself feeling bad for the brother, who clearly loved the place and spent each day working hard to keep everything going.

"And he'd never do anything like this," Quentin spread his hands out to encompass the office. "Not only do I look after the horses, but I'm the Estate Manager. I deal with the tenant farms and farmers, rental properties, balance the books, sort out repairs on the house. God knows what'll happen to the place once Clive gets his hands on it." Quentin ran his hands through his dirty blond hair, combing it off his forehead with his fingers. A muscle in his jaw ticked and he appeared to be grinding his teeth together.

"What was it like growing up with him?" Anderson asked, clearly trying to deflect the man's anger away from the estate and its problems and get the questioning back on track.

"He was always a bit of a golden boy, very popular at school. Well he would be wouldn't he with his inheritance behind him."

Crane could hear the bitterness in Quentin's voice. "You weren't then?" he asked.

"No, second in line doesn't get much attention. Number one son has it all."

Anderson said, "Isn't that a bit archaic?"

"Very, but what can you do? I expect I'll be kept on in some sort of estate manager role and have to be beholden to my brother for every penny he deigns to throw my way."

"Well," Anderson said, standing. "Thanks very much for your time. Just in case," he handed Quentin a card, "call me if you see Janey, or hear anything about her whereabouts."

Crane and Anderson walked out of the office and retraced their footsteps around to the front of the house. As they climbed into the car, Crane said, "He really does hate his brother and Janey doesn't he?"

"It seems that way. But does he hate them enough to do something to Janey?"

Thirteen

Crane had just walked into the kitchen and was looking forward to breakfast as he joined his wife Tina. His son Daniel was happily munching his way through a chocolate cereal, most of which seemed to be smeared across the toddler's face. At the sight of his father, he gave a toothy grin and waved his spoon around, which meant that chocolate coloured milk ended up all over the kitchen cupboards like some sort of arterial spray. Shaking the gory thought out of his head, Crane turned his attention to the news programme on the portable TV which was tucked into the space under the wall mounted cupboards and the kitchen counter.

"Good morning and welcome to Breakfast. Our top story this morning, super model Janey Carlton has been reported missing. She was last seen at her home in Farnham 36 hours ago. Her husband, Major Clive Cunningham, currently serving with the British Army and based at Aldershot Garrison, hasn't been seen in public since her disappearance but is understood to be devastated and desperate for her to get in touch. The couple were last seen together at a restaurant in Farnham, the night before last and our reporter is there for us now."

"Jesus Christ," Crane said, "that's all we bloody need."

"Tom," Tina hissed. "Daniel," and she nodded in the direction of their son.

"Sorry, love." Crane knew Tina didn't like him blaspheming or swearing in front of Daniel. But, hey, at least he hadn't said the 'f' word, which is what he'd felt like uttering, in deference to his son's presence in the kitchen.

"Bad news then?" she asked, grasping her long dark hair in her hands, pulling it behind her head and securing it with a hair band from around her wrist.

Crane took a moment to appreciate his wife. She'd suffered from a bad bout of post natal depression a couple of years ago, after the birth of Daniel and Crane had been very worried about her. At the time she'd lost all her self-esteem, couldn't seem to shake the weight accumulated during her pregnancy and generally couldn't cope with looking after the house, the baby and herself. But those dark days were behind them now and Tina was glowing with heath. Her long dark hair shone in the overhead lights, her trim figure was outlined by leggings and a tee-shirt and her eyes were clear and inquisitive. He'd often pondered the idea of having a second child, but always shied away from discussing it with her. The last thing he wanted to do was to re-awaken the spectre of Tina's depression.

"Someone's leaked the story to the press about Janey Cunningham," he said. "We were trying to keep a lid on it for now. Bugger."

"Tom!"

Crane looked at her and could only hope this phase of hers about watching his language around their son would pass quickly. He knew from past experience she'd soon move on to another aspect of their son's development that she wanted him to pay attention to.

"Got to go, love, sorry," and he kissed her cheek, ruffled Daniel's hair and was gone before she could rebuke him for not eating anything before leaving the house.

As he backed the car off the drive of their army quarter, one of a row of smart, modern, three bedroomed detached houses on Aldershot Garrison, the radio informed him:

"Model Janey Carlton, the face of Lasting Cosmetics, is understood to have been missing for 36 hours. Her career began when she was discovered as a young girl of 17 and she has had a stellar career over the past 30 years. She was often hailed as 'the new Twiggy' and has long been regarded as one of Britain's most professional of the super models. We had hoped to get a statement from the family, but her Agent Laura Battle spoke for them when she said, "We are all devastated by Janey's disappearance. We are praying for her safe return."

Crane turned the radio off as he drove down Hospital Hill and then onward around the town centre, up towards Aldershot Police Station, feeling like a cartoon character with steam puffing out of his ears. His boss, Captain Draper, wouldn't be happy about this. He would be shouted at by those officers above him and he, in turn, would shout at those below him, which meant Crane.

Crane found Anderson in his office surrounded by newspapers. It was clear Anderson was not taking the publicity well either, as there were no biscuits in the saucer of his cup of tea, not even a crumb. It must be bad for Anderson's liking for sweet biscuits and cakes to disappear. His sweet tooth was legendary and the bottom drawer of his desk normally held some treat or other.

"What the hell is all this?" he asked Crane, shaking the front page of one of the papers. "Who leaked it?"

"Christ knows," said Crane. "But on the TV they were reporting from the restaurant in Farnham, so they would be my best guess. They might have heard something on the local gossip grapevine. It wouldn't take much investigative work, I suppose," he said. "All it would need would be for one or two of Janey's friends in town who'd received a phone call from the Major asking where his wife was, being overhead whilst having coffee and discussing her disappearance. Then, as their restaurant was the last place the Cunninghams were seen, well the free publicity for them would be too tempting I should think. It wouldn't be anyone from my office… and not yours," he quickly added at a glare from Anderson.

Crane picked up one of the papers, which carried a full length picture of Janey Carlton advertising an alluring perfume, as the phone on Anderson's desk rang.

Listening for a moment, Anderson said, "Good morning, Major Cunningham. Sgt Major Crane is with me, so I'm going to put you on speaker," ignoring Crane's frantic hand signals, as he was trying to indicate he didn't want to speak to the Major.

"Good morning, sir," Crane said and glared at Anderson.

"What the hell is going on, Crane? There are reporters at the end of the drive, my father is being harassed and I've had to turn off my mobile phone as it won't stop ringing with calls from the press. I thought no one was supposed to know about Janey yet?"

"They weren't, sir, but I can assure you the leak didn't come from the military police, or the Aldershot police."

"Well who did it come from?"

"We think the restaurant in Farnham," said Anderson. "I've got a patrol car on its way to clear the reporters from there and have a word with the owners."

"I tell you I'm not happy about this, not happy at all. I'll be having words with your Captain, Crane."

"You are quite within your rights to do that, of course," Anderson said, "but it might be more productive to work with us, not against us, sir."

"What the hell do you mean?" Cunningham's anger could be heard crackling down the line like a bolt of lightning fizzing in the night sky.

"Have you any idea where Janey might have gone, sir?" said Crane. "Is there anywhere else that you haven't told us about that she likes to go to? Or are there any friends that she might be staying with?"

"Look, Anderson," the Major said, effectively ignoring Crane, which was fine by him, "I've told you all I know. The rest is up to you. And if you don't find her, I'll be having a word with your superiors as well!"

"Major…"

But Cunningham cut across Anderson. "It's your job to find her, not mine, so I suggest you get on with it!" and the telephone receiver was replaced with such force it made Crane wince.

"Not a happy bunny then," Anderson said.

"You know, Derek, I do wish bloody officers would work with me, not against me. All they do is shout and threaten, instead of discussing and helping. It drives me up the wall."

Just then someone appeared with a welcome black

coffee for Crane. As he took the mug he said to Derek, "What's our next move?"

"Battle."

"Eh?" Crane looked at Anderson over the rim of the mug.

"Laura Battle. You thought she knew more than she was letting on yesterday, so I think it's time to put more pressure on her. Come one," and Anderson stood and grabbed his raincoat from the coat stand in the corner of his office. Looking longingly at the coffee mug he had to leave behind, Crane followed his friend out of the door.

Fourteen

As expected, Laura Battle was no more pleased to see Crane and Anderson than she had been yesterday. But this time Crane sensed a chink in her hardened persona. It was in the slight trembling of her hands and the excessive blinking. The cigarette she was smoking was being quickly sucked out of existence.

"Janey's been missing for nearly 48 hours," Crane said, once they were settled on the settees again. "We really need your help, Ms Battle."

"I don't see how I can help," she said. "I've told you…"

Anderson cut across her protestations. "Look, if you really are the friend to Janey that you say you are, please help us find her."

Laura Battle turned away from Anderson to stare out of the window.

"Between you and me, I'm beginning to get a bit worried," Anderson said.

Her head shot around.

"It's been two nights since she was last seen, well, normally that means…"

Crane looked at Laura Battle closely as Anderson didn't complete his sentence.

"What?" she asked. "What does that 'normally' mean?"

"We're afraid she might be dead," Crane said.

"Dead! What are you talking about? Why would she be dead?" The prospect of the death of her friend clearly horrified Laura Battle. Her eyes bulged and she frantically stubbed out her cigarette in a nearby ashtray.

"We don't know, but we suspect you might," said Crane. "Was there something, or someone she was involved with, that no one wants to tell us about? Was she involved with, say, unsavoury people or went to places with a dodgy reputation?"

"You can't protect her anymore, Laura," said Anderson. "Help us to help her. Is there anything, anything at all you can tell us?"

Laura stood and walked over to the window, staring out across her Japanese garden and lit yet another cigarette. Turning back she blew out a lungful of smoke and said, "Sex games."

Crane caught Derek's eye. That was a new one on him and also on Derek by the look on his face.

"What are you talking about?"

"Janey and Clive belong to a private club in Mayfair. It's near their London home."

"Why on earth didn't you tell us about this yesterday?"

"Because no one was supposed to know. I don't think Clive knows that I know. It was a secret, because of who she was, I mean is."

"But couldn't one of the, um, clientele, leak the information to the press," said Crane.

"No, no one would dare. Everyone who goes there has one reason or another for keeping their activities secret."

"So they're all rich." Crane shook his head, having had past experience of those with power and money who think they can do what they want, when they want and to whom they want, without any comeback at all.

"Very. You can't get if in you're not. Do you think someone there might have, might have…?" tears filled Laura's eyes and Crane saw through her hardness and glimpsed the feelings she had for her friend beneath the hardened face she presented to the world.

"We don't know, but it's a start," said Anderson. "Right, I need the name of the club and what were you saying about a London house?"

It hadn't taken Crane and Anderson long to drive from Reading to Farnham. They'd considered phoning Major Cunningham beforehand, but Crane much preferred to see the look on his face when he realised that they knew all about his dirty little secret activities. And Crane wasn't disappointed. The Major had been all bluff and bluster when they confronted him with their knowledge of their membership of the sex club in Mayfair.

"I haven't the faintest idea what you're talking about," was his retort. "Look, have you nothing better to do than listen to gossip? My wife has been missing for nearly 48 hours and I've heard little in the way of progress from either of you. And now you have the temerity to accuse me, a Major in the British Army, of belonging to some sort of sordid club. I've a good mind to report you both to your superiors."

"You can stop that now, Major," said Crane.

"I beg your pardon?"

"I said you can stop that. Pulling rank won't work with us. I couldn't give a toss what your rank is and to be honest I couldn't give a toss about you. But what I do care about is finding your wife."

"You can't get away with speaking to me like this!" Clearly the Major hadn't come across anyone like Crane before. His face turned puce and his fists clenched at his side.

"Major, I can speak to you however I wish. You're the one that has been obstructing our enquiries by withholding what could turn out to be vital information."

Major Cunningham stared at Anderson, the flush of anger still visible on his face and neck. "What are you going to do about him?" he demanded, pointing at Crane. "Are you going to let him talk to me like that?"

"Yes," replied Anderson. "Sgt Major Crane here is quite right in his assertions. So, tell us all about this club you and your wife belong to, Major Cunningham. Oh, and while you're at it, we need the address of your property in London and the keys. You know, the house you also forgot to mention. I really would advise co-operation, Major."

Cunningham stared at the two men for a moment, before sinking into a chair and burying his face in his hands.

Fifteen

…Once his real identity was cloaked in anonymity and his ill-gotten gains at a suitable level, he vacated his housing association flat. Not wanting to take with him anything of his former life, he left the flat fully furnished. As he closed the front door for the final time, he grabbed a passing kid and paid him to deliver an envelope to the offices of the association. He never did know who opened the envelope which contained nothing more than a key with a tag on it. Written on that tag was the address of the property. He'd checked a few months later, watching his old home from a safe distance and was pleased to discover a new tenant living there. His bridges had been burned. No one would find him now.

Under a carefully constructed false identity he had purchased a secluded house in the area near Hampstead Heath in London, from an on-line colleague who had fallen on hard times. The price was laughably low, but then that was the way of the world. Money makes money and he was only too happy to take advantage of the man's fall onto hard times, paying less than 50% of its true worth. His colleague needed money quickly and he had it. It was a doddle to arrange payment and he used an on-line firm of solicitors to handle the legalities.

Once he'd settled in, his investigations into his mother's life were ramped up. He firstly gathered as much historical information on her as he could, from her fairy tale beginning when she was spotted whilst out shopping with friends, to her current modelling assignments and her marriage to a Major in the British Army.

Janey Carlton, super model. His mother.

As he turned over in his mind his options, he decided it was best to bide his time, while he watched her. Sometimes this was from afar, via the internet and television, whilst at other times he was near enough to touch her, as he watched from the crowd lining the red carpet at a film premier. He was waiting for a suitable opening so he could inveigle himself into her life. But it would have to be a subtle and natural meeting.

If he was going to move in those rarefied circles he needed a lifestyle that would give the impression that he was one of them. One of the beautiful people who appeared to have no worries other than how to fill their leisure hours. How to keep raising the bar on excitement, so as not to get bored, jaded and become yesterday's news.

In order to attain those lofty heights, he ramped up his on-line activities. Some hackers were in it for the notoriety, not the money, wanting to be known as the man or woman who hacked into GCHQ or the Pentagon. That was, to him, a waste of talent and a waste of time. By all means hack into difficult targets, but for goodness sake once in there, steal something that someone wants and then sell it to the highest bidder. Or hack to order. But never, never, do it for jollies. That path was for the stupid geeks who couldn't see further than their keyboard and were trapped in their bedsitting rooms. They were like vampires, only venturing out at night and then only when it was absolutely necessary. After a few audacious hacks, which he never publicised or told anyone about, he had amassed enough money to project the illusion he was seeking.

He had kept up his pursuit of the perfect body and now had enviable pecks and abs, beautifully tailored clothes and a suitably trendy, not to mention very expensive, haircut. It was a carefully arranged shaggy cut that gave him a smouldering look; his dark eyes and dark hair presumably a gift from his unknown father. A tangled relationship with some airhead girl was the last thing he wanted, but he needed someone on his arm, so he paid for escorts to accompany him, as he began to appear at the restaurants and clubs frequented by Janey and her husband. He took holidays when and where they did. When they were comfortable seeing him as part of their social set, he would be ready to make his move.

Sixteen

Notting Hill was not an area Crane was familiar with. He and Anderson had gone directly from Farnham and wound their way along the M3 and M4 motorways before heading into Central London. A ride around the outskirts of Hyde Park brought them to the an area of London famous for the Notting Hill Carnival, which was a huge street party held over two days in August, with the focus being on a celebration of all things Caribbean. As a result, Crane wasn't prepared for what he saw. He'd expected a seedy area, but instead saw clean bright streets with elegant rows of Georgian houses fronted by porticos and columns, three and four storeys high. In some streets they were painted bright, deep colours. Terracotta, blue and green hues dominated the rows of houses around Portobello Market, but as they turned into the street they were looking for Crane was relieved to see pastel coloured buildings, which were more pleasing to the eye, interspersed with the original white.

Anderson managed to park the car in a tight space and after feeding the parking meter, they walked a few doors down to number 53. Crane took a few steps back to stand against the edge of the pavement in order to view the full house. Including the basement it was five storeys high, an imposing sight in anyone's book. He wondered at the cost of such a property, a whole house mind, not broken up into flats, and realised it must be in the millions. He suspected that the property had been in the family for years. If not, running a large estate in the country must be a very profitable venture indeed.

As they walked up to the front door, Crane fished the keys out of his pocket, but Anderson touched Crane's arm to stop him putting the key into the lock.

"We ought to make sure there's no one in first," he said.

Crane nodded and proceeded to jingle them in his hand, while they waited for an answer to their knock on the door.

Crane was itching to get inside and was just about to give up and open the door anyway, when they heard the sound of locks being undone behind the door. It opened to reveal an older man, with a military bearing, immaculately groomed. Crane was just about to ask if he was Lord Garford, when he took a closer look at how the man was dressed. He was in dark trousers with matching waistcoat over a white shirt and muted tie. Not much different to Crane's attire really, but Crane was no one's servant, which is what he suspected the man in front of them was.

"Good afternoon," Crane said. "Is Lord Garford in?"

The man said, "Who shall I say is calling?"

"DI Anderson and Sgt Major Crane, SIB," and Crane held up his ID and nudged Derek to do the same.

"Very well, sirs, please follow me," and they walked behind him into a cool hallway, with a beautiful original tiled floor, something Crane had in his Victorian terraced house in Aldershot, which was currently rented out. Only this hallway was substantially bigger, with more rooms off the long corridor and a much, much bigger stairway leading upstairs. They were shown into what appeared to be a study and asked to wait while Lord Garford was summoned.

"How do we play this?" Crane asked Anderson after the manservant had left.

"Carefully," Anderson said. "You might not like the aristocracy, but trust me, life will be a lot more pleasant for us if we don't step on his toes. Just try and be polite, even if you can't be deferential."

"You have a very low opinion of me, Derek," Crane said.

"Born of knowing you well," Anderson grinned. "So behave yourself."

"Yes, Detective Inspector," Crane quipped and had to suffer a thump on the arm from Anderson in retaliation.

It was then that the door opened and the person Crane presumed to be Lord Garford entered the room. He was dressed remarkably similar to his son, Major Cunningham. Both had that studied casual way of dressing that was anything but. He wore buff coloured trousers without a wrinkle to be seen in them, a soft cotton chequered shirt and muddy coloured tie. He walked towards them without speaking and moved to sit behind his desk. He indicated the two vacant chairs in front of it and Crane and Anderson sat. Personally Crane thought it extremely rude of the man not to introduce himself and to shake their hands and he wanted to wipe the stare of disdain he was having to endure from Lord Garford, off the man's smug softjawed face. Garford's small chin was becoming lost in jowls that hung around his neck. His piggy eyes and thinning hair completed the undesirable looking face.

"Good afternoon, sir," began Anderson. "As you may know, Sgt Major Crane and I are investigating the disappearance of your daughter in law, Janey Cunningham."

Lord Garford nodded his head and said, "My son rang me to tell me you were on your way. Although I don't see what you expect to find in my house that would help your investigation."

Anderson ignored the implied question and said, "We understand that your son and his wife stay here when they are in London, which is quite often."

"They do. But I still fail to see why you are here."

"Are you aware that your son has given his permission for us to look through the house, to see if we could find anything that would help our investigation?"

"Do you have a search warrant?"

"Not at this stage, sir. As I said, your son has given us permission to be here."

Lord Garford looked at them for a moment, then said, "Very well, but I will only permit you to look in his rooms."

"His rooms?" Crane asked. He'd been expecting the Cunninghams to use one of the bedrooms in the house, of which he was sure there were many.

"Yes, they use the basement when they stay here. You'll find that the keys he gave you are for the front door of the basement flat, so I'll thank you to come with me and pursue your investigation downstairs."

Lord Garford walked out of the study with the air of a man who was used to being followed and led them back out of the front door and proceeded down the stone steps to the basement. Standing aside, he let Anderson faff about with the keys, until he found the correct one and opened the door. Lord Garford followed them in.

Crane was about to ask Lord Garford to wait for them outside, when he saw the steely look of determination on the old man's face. So instead he said, "Perhaps you'd like to wait here, sir," he said, indicating a settee in the large lounge area they'd walked into.

The apartment, instead of being dark and gloomy as Crane perceived a basement to be, was filled with light. The large lounge area led into a dining area, with a large black glass table that seated eight. Beyond that was the kitchen, with black gloss cupboards, white tiles on the wall and on the floor. The impression was one of style, comfort and screamed money. A bank of glass curtains showcased a beautiful cottage type garden, furnished with the obligatory outdoor settees, coffee tables and sun loungers. One wall of the dining area was arched and through that arch Crane found two bedrooms with a bathroom between them. Crane took the bedrooms and Anderson the lounge. Crane felt it was safer that Anderson poke about in front of Lord Garford, for Crane couldn't guarantee to keep his mouth shut if his Lordship decided to interfere.

One bedroom was in the front of the house and clearly set out as a guest bedroom. All the cupboards and drawers were empty. There was nothing under the huge bed and nothing hidden in the pile of pillows and cushions that adorned the top of it. Crane was careful to put them back as he'd found them. The second bedroom, which backed onto the garden, was far more interesting. It was clearly Major and Mrs Cunningham's bedroom, as this time the cupboards were full of clothes and shoes. Nothing there was of any interest, even though Crane went through all the handbags and shoe boxes Janey Cunningham had accumulated. Crane wondered how many handbags and shoes a woman needed, especially as this was a second home. It was clear to him that she needed the trappings of wealth to validate her as a person, which was really sad. But he guessed it went with the nervous traits of not eating much and smoking too much, that Laura Battle had told them about.

When Crane reached the bedside cabinets, things got more interesting. For they were both locked. Finding Anderson sorting through the kitchen cupboards, he grabbed the keys from him and went back to unlock what he hoped were the secrets of Janey Cunningham's life.

Seventeen

Crane walked back into lounge with a couple of pieces of papers in his hand and showed them to Anderson. Whilst Anderson was reading them, Lord Garford said, "What it is? What have you found?"

Crane didn't reply, just watched Anderson read the two pieces of paper. When Anderson had finished, he raised his head and said, "I'm not sure this information should be shared at the moment, sir."

"Well I'm bloody sure it should. You're in my house. You found the papers in my house. Now tell me what they say."

Lord Garford had stood up and was clearly expecting Anderson to comply his with request. Well, to be fair it was more of a demand, really. Crane kept his own counsel and waited as well.

"Very well, sir, perhaps you be good enough to sit down."

Mollified, Lord Garford complied, never taking his eyes off Anderson, as though frightened the policeman would change his mind.

"This one," Anderson held one sheet of paper aloft, "is confirmation that your son and his wife are members of the Mayfair Club."

As the colour drained out of the old man's face, it was clear he understood what that meant. "That can't be right," he said.

"I'm afraid it is, sir, here," and Anderson handed the paper to the man who suddenly looked like the old man he was, not a peer of the realm.

"I take it you understand what this means, sir," Crane said. "According to the literature I found, it seems the Mayfair Club is for 'swingers' for want of a better description."

Lord Garford nodded his reply. He cleared his throat and said, "I know, Crane. Not that I ever joined, but, well, I know of people who did. It's been going for quite some years now. I never thought Clive and Janey would be into any of that, though," and he closed his eyes against the words on the paper. "I always thought they were happily married. That they each gave the other all they needed, but it appears not." After a moment's pause he said, "What's on the other one?"

Anderson duly passed the paper over. "It seems Mrs Cunningham has a bank account that no one knows about. The balance, when it was opened, was several thousand pounds, but that was over three years ago, so at the moment I've no idea what this means."

"Where did you find it?" Lord Garford looked at Crane.

"Hidden in a false cupboard in the bathroom, so it was clearly something Janey didn't want anyone to know about."

"So, you've already uncovered secrets, lies and undisclosed money. I thought I knew Clive, and Janey come to that, but it appears not. Do you think any of this is connected to her disappearance?"

"At this moment I'm not sure of anything, sir. But the club and the bank account are leads that we need to follow-up," said Anderson.

"Of course," Lord Garford nodded. "Will you keep me informed?"

"Naturally," Anderson agreed. "Where will you be, sir?"

"Here in London, at least until the end of the week, obligations in the House of Lords and all that."

"Very well," said Anderson and the three men turned and left the basement flat.

When they reached the pavement, Crane watched Lord Garford climb the few steps to his front door, with a heavy tread and a slump to his shoulders that hadn't been there when they'd arrived.

Crane didn't much like ruining people's lives like that, but then, he consoled himself, he wasn't really the one doing it. If people didn't do such things, or kept such awful secrets from their families, then his job would be a lot easier.

"I didn't enjoy that," said Crane to Anderson as they pulled away from the house.

"Neither did I," said Anderson, "but what else could we do? He did insist on being told."

"Oh well," said Crane, "Let's hope that's the worst of it."

As it was early evening, Crane and Anderson decided to drive to the Mayfair Club, to see what they could find out there, before returning to Aldershot. They found a nearby coffee shop, where Crane filled up his caffeine tank and they both called their wives, telling them they wouldn't be home for a while yet. Both women received the news stoically, as if to say, what's new?

What was new to Crane and Anderson was a swingers club such as the Mayfair. Anderson's warrant card gained them entry past a bemused doorman. Upon asking to speak to the manager, they were led down a thickly carpeted hallway and down a set of stairs into a basement, which was clearly a no go area for clients. The basement was sparsely furnished, money obviously being better spent upstairs and as they entered it, a man came up to them, one hand held out.

"Good evening, gentlemen," he said. "I'm Dante Skinner. How can I help you?"

Crane introduced them both and wanted to know who Skinner was. "Are you the manager, sir?" he asked.

"Owner, actually," and Skinner ran his perfectly manicured fingers through his beautifully styled dark hair, all gel and lacquer Crane thought as he saw the way it glinted in the overhead lights.

"I thought the club had been going for many years?" Crane asked.

"Oh, it has, 30 years to be exact. My father founded the club and I've taken over as the old man has retired."

That explained the Skinner bit of the name but Dante? So Crane asked.

"My mother is Italian, what can I say?" Skinner smiled and now Crane could see indicators of his heritage. The jet black hair, slightly olive skin and tall frame.

"What sort of club is this precisely, sir?" Anderson asked.

"A club where people can come and drink and meet people with similar tastes, in a protected and confidential environment." Which was exactly the strap line on the membership papers they'd found in the basement flat.

"A knocking shop," said Crane, deliberately being provocative.

But it seemed Dante Skinner was too smooth to be riled and he laughed at Crane's description of his club. "So, what brings you here?" Dante said. "You're a long way from Aldershot."

Anderson explained that they were investigating the disappearance of Janey Cunningham, who was a member with her husband, Major Cunningham.

"Yes," Dante mused. "I saw that on the news. But why are you talking to me? I can't help you."

"Yes you can," Crane decided to drop the 'sir' bollocks. He was getting tired and was fed up with people not giving them information. "Is there a couple they were particularly friendly with? Anyone they socialised with regularly?"

"Look, Sgt Major isn't it? This is a private members' club. The emphasis being on the word private, so unless you have a warrant…" Dante let his hand hang in the air.

"Please, sir," Anderson said. "Can't we do this civilly, without the need for warrants and all that sort of stuff?"

Dante looked puzzled. "What sort of stuff?"

"Well, we would have good grounds for closing you down for a while, for say, obstructing an investigation."

"Or," joined in Crane, "we could treat this as a crime scene and shut the whole place for, well, who knows how long? Some investigations take months. All it would take is a quick call to the Metropolitan Police. Don't you agree, Derek?"

"Definitely, Crane," Anderson confirmed.

Dante Skinner paled under his olive toned skin and ran his fingers through his hair again. But still he hesitated.

"Please, Mr Skinner. A woman is missing. A woman who was, I assume a regular at your club."

Dante nodded his agreement.

"So, won't you help us? Is there anything you can tell us that might move the case forward? All we want are the names of those couples the Cunningham's were particularly friendly with."

"We don't have to tell anyone that the information came from you. We'll protect your precious privacy policy," Crane said still trying his best to persuade the man to co-operate.

Skinner pulled out a packet of Dunhill cigarettes and lit one with a gold lighter. After he'd blown out the smoke he said, "Cynthia and Justin Hall. I understand they've become quite close to the Cunninghams. They live in Kensington. I'm sure you can find them, after all you are policemen," and he gave a wry smile.

"Thank you, Mr Skinner," said Anderson. "We'll not take up any more of your time," at which Skinner looked relieved.

"But don't worry, we'll be in touch if we need to know anything else," said Crane and winked at Dante Skinner, before they climbed the stairs back to street level, leaving the club owner to his secrets.

Eighteen

...It had been a few days since he had been in the house, other demands on his time meant that he had been unable to continue his surveillance until this evening. As he watched the family leave for an outing to the cinema, talking loudly about which film they were about to see and where to go afterwards for something to eat, he left his car which was parked a few houses further down the street. Their chatter continued as he walked towards them. As their words and laughter enveloped him, tendrils of their talk pricked at his arms like a thousand needles. Jealousy threatened to overwhelm him as he watched Tyler with his perfect family. Tyler, who had good job, nice car, beautiful wife, and the obligatory 2.4 children. Whilst he, well he had not been so lucky. His life had taken a different path.

Shaking himself like a dog wanting to shed water from his coat, so that drops of his envy splattered around his feet, he slapped his own face, forcing himself to get his emotions under control. He reminded himself that he was the one in the position of power, not Tyler. And that in time, well, Tyler would get what he deserved.

Once again he got into the house easily enough. The parcel tucked under his arm rustled as he squeezed through the door in the dark, not wanting to open it wide in case it drew anyone's attention. He prowled through the ground floor by the slim beam of his torch, checking that he really was alone and silently thanking the family for closing the curtains before they had left. Satisfied, he put the parcel down on the hall table and proceeded to poke about. The downstairs of the property had clearly been renovated, that much was visible from his torch. No lights had been left on, so he moved through the rooms like the prowler he was, quickly and quietly, trying not to leave anything of himself behind. His hands were covered with surgical gloves and his shoes had paper slip-overs on. He lifted photographs in silver frames from the furniture they rested on, looking at the family pictures, which appeared to have been snapped during various holidays. He ran his torch over the paintings on the wall. They were okay, but a bit too abstract for his taste. Modern art wasn't something he understood or felt an affinity for.

The kitchen was all designer cupboards and marble worktops, with a free-standing island complete with high stools, where presumably the family could chat while the cooking took place, or gather around for a quick breakfast before starting their day. Oh yes, Tyler Wells had clearly done very well for himself.

Towards the back of the house, he found a space that had a completely different atmosphere. Most of the rooms he'd been in had evidence of people leading busy lives, with toys, books and magazines strewn around. It was as if the house was quietly waiting for the owners to return and pick up the discarded books, to carrying on reading the next chapter. He'd looked at Penny's magazines, Vogue, Tattler, Homes and Gardens, all clear indicators of her expensive ways and good taste. In his mind's eye he could see her wandering into the lounge with a cup of coffee, ready to read an article about this season's must have designer handbag.

The final room on the ground floor was completely different in furnishing and feeling. Tyler's study was clearly a male space, all dark furniture, cabinets and desk. There was nothing out of place here. The desk had a laptop on it and nothing else.

He moved around the desk, pulled out the leather office chair and sat, taking a moment to settle into the chair, pulling Tyler's life around him like a well-worn overcoat. Then he reached out and opened the laptop. As he clicked the icon in the middle of the screen, the operating system came to life and granted him access. No password. How trusting. He settled down to his mischief, occasionally reaching into desk drawers or moving over to the filing cabinet, to obtain the information he needed.

His mission complete, he walked back through the house, collecting the package he had left in the hallway. Mounting the stairs, a sense of urgency in his stride as he needed to be away before the family arrived back, he walked into Tyler and Penny's bedroom. Taking a moment to work out which was Penny's side of the bed, he then put a single red rose on her pillow. That was his calling card for this evening. A blood red rose that would send the message to Tyler that he was being watched.

With a smile on his face, he left the house, wishing he could see Tyler's expression when he saw the bloom.

.

Nineteen

The girls tumbled through the front door. Tyler often thought that they never walked anywhere, they were always on the run, always trying to outdo each other, to be the first in the door, up the stairs, to the dining table. He smiled at their antics as Penny shushed them up the stairs to get ready for bed. As he walked into the lounge, their laughter floated down the stairs; it was a perfect end to a perfect evening. The new Cinderella film by Kenneth Branagh had been a huge hit, not only with the girls, but with him and Penny also. It was a heart-warming tale of love and triumph over adversity. He felt the new mantra in the house was going to be, 'Have courage and be kind,' Cinderella's mother's last words to her beautiful daughter.

Whilst he waited for Penny, he turned on the television to watch the late evening news. The top story, in fact the only story really, was the disappearance of well-known model Janey Carlton. The media were reporting from outside her house, outside her agent's house and anywhere else they could think of that had even a tenuous connection to the missing model. Then the news anchor settled down to a longer piece, interviewing a former police detective. What had really happened to Janey Carlton? Their speculation went on and on.... Kidnap, (but there had been no ransom demand that they were aware of), murder (where was her body), she may have left her husband (who for), she could have simply just disappeared for a while (a la Agatha Christie who disappeared for 11 days back in the 1920's). The news anchor said that Janey's husband was distraught and beyond consolation. The policeman explained that as her husband was a major in the British Army, the case was no doubt being investigated by both the civilian and the military police.

As they launched into an explanation of how the two police forces worked together, Tyler stopped listening and wondered what it would be like if Penny went missing? How would he feel? Somehow 'distraught' didn't seem to even come close. He was practically pole-axed with fear just speculating about it. Maybe it was because he was an adopted child that he needed such commitment and reassurance in his personal life. Losing Penny would be like cutting off his arm. Losing his children would be like cutting off the other one. Losing his adoptive parents would be like a hammer blow that would take months, if not years, to come to terms with. Battling the fear that threatened to consume him, Tyler went through to the kitchen to see Penny. He needed reassurance that she was really there, he needed to touch her and kiss her. He needed to ground himself.

He found her making a cup of tea and standing behind her, he put his arms around her waist.

"Hey," she said, "what a lovely evening that was. Although I think I ate too much pizza. I'm so full I'm going to pop!"

"Your stomach feels fine to me," he said running his hands over it.

"Oh, I forgot to thank you," she said stirring the tea.

"Thank me for what?"

"For making the bed and leaving sexy underwear out for me to wear the other morning. I felt horny all day. And now you've left a rose on my pillow! I never knew you were such a romantic." Penny turned in his arms and kissed him deeply.

Tyler did his best to respond, but he wasn't turned on by her kiss, rather turned off, as a shiver ran down his back, for he had done no such thing. He hadn't left out any underwear for her one morning. To be frank, he was always far too intent on getting to the office in the mornings, than thinking of sex. As for a rose, what bloody rose?

He pulled away from Penny and said, "Where's that tea? I'm dying of thirst," and laughed to distract her from further conversation about his so called 'gifts'.

As they walked back into the lounge, he debated telling her that it wasn't him who had left out the underwear and put a red rose on her pillow. But to be honest, he didn't want to frighten her. It was probably nothing, he decided. Just a prank. Maybe it was the girls messing about? Yes, he thought, taking a sip of his tea. The girls are the best explanation. But then he thought back to the phone calls in the office. The ones where no one was there when he answered. Perhaps he needed to start taking some notice of what and who was around him. Could it be that a stalker was watching them and that he had somehow gained access to the house? Tyler went cold to the core of his being, as if someone had just walked over his grave. The words, 'Have courage and be kind', flitted through his mind.

He needed to find the courage to deal with this and get to the bottom of it, and be kind to Penny and the girls by not burdening them with his fears. But was he up to the job?

Twenty

"Okay, Crane," Draper said, looking at the white boards in the open plan SIB office that detailed the investigation into the disappearance of Janey Cunningham, "Where do we stand?" He was dressed in fatigues and struck a relaxed pose, propped up on the side of a desk with his hands in his pockets.

"Well, at the moment, sir, it's more a case of what we don't know, than what we do know."

"Explain."

"Well," Crane scratched at his black curly hair, "We don't know where she is, we don't know what's happened to her and we don't know who did whatever has been done to her. We still don't know if it's a disappearance, a kidnap, or a murder and if it is a murder then why haven't we found the body. We now know what Major and Mrs Cunningham got up to in their private life and to be honest, boss, I get the feeling we've only just scratched the surface on that one."

Draper sighed. "I suspect you're right. What are you and Anderson up to today?"

"We're off to interview the couple from the swingers' club. We've made an appointment with them, so it's not going to be a wild goose chase."

Draper smiled, "You sure about that, Crane?"

Crane returned the grin. "To be bloody honest, boss, I'm not sure of anything. Talk about going with the flow. Every time I lift up a corner of the Cunningham's lives, I find something new that's even more bizarre than the previous fact. How are they taking it up there?" Crane was alluding to Major Cunningham's and Draper's superiors.

"Not well at all. He's been officially suspended until the case is brought to some sort of conclusion. The rumour mill is working overtime and he's becoming a bit of a joke amongst the soldiers he commands. So the brass are working on damage limitation at the moment. To be honest, even if he comes out of this in the clear, I suspect he'll be moved on to somewhere faraway, where hopefully the rumours won't have spread to, if he isn't persuaded to resign, that is."

"Poor bugger." For once Crane had some sympathy for the man, if he was innocent that was, and he unconsciously scratched at the scar under his short beard as he thought about it.

"It's not the way the men upstairs see it," said Draper. "They feel he should have had more control over his wife."

Crane smiled ruefully, "Typical senior officer attitude."

"Well, as far as they are concerned, Janey Cunningham, or Carlton, or whatever you want to call her, represented the British Army just as much as her husband. And disappearing is not in the handbook. So," Draper pushed himself off the desk, "no pressure, but an early resolution to this mess would be appreciated. What we really need to do is to find Janey Cunningham, preferably alive."

"Don't I know it, boss. She's like a phantom, a will-o'-the-wisp, protected by her friend Laura Battle. That woman is doing my head in, she's lied to us twice already, let's hope that's the last of them."

"Keep me posted, Crane," said Draper as he walked away. "And remember," he turned back "an officer who has killed his wife isn't what the brass want to hear. But just in case he has, they're backing away from him, distancing themselves already. You can be sure they'll be quick to disown him if he has."

Draper raised his hand in farewell, as he pushed out of the office door.

Twenty One

Crane wasn't sure what to expect of a couple who enjoyed having sex with other people, but Cynthia and Justin Hall were definitely not it. Crane put Justin Hall at mid-forties. He was a bit myopic, his left eye wandering at times, as though it had a life of its own. Cynthia, of a similar age, brought to mind a horse, her neighing laugh grating on Crane's already frayed nerves. How anyone could find them even remotely attractive was beyond Crane. Perhaps it didn't matter so much if you were high on drink or drugs, but still, the thought of seeing the Hall's with no clothes on… well it was best not to go there. He tried hard to concentrate on what Anderson was saying.

"So, you admit to knowing Major and Mrs Cunningham, through the Mayfair Club?" Anderson asked the couple, who were sat side by side on the sofa in the lounge of their London home.

"Yes," Justin Hall replied.

"And you know them well?"

Hall had the grace to blush, a flush high on his cheek bones. "Well, yes, I suppose so."

"We weren't really friends, though," said Cynthia.

"No?" asked Crane.

"Well, no," she replied. "We only met them at the club, never outside."

"Oh, so no dinner parties, days out, drinks here and there, nothing like that?"

"No," she shook her head vigorously, her mane of reddish brown hair swinging backwards and forwards.

"So they were nothing more than regular sex partners?"

"That's right," she said with some satisfaction, making Crane think that the Halls were desperate to distance themselves from the Major and his wife.

"Have you ever been to their home?"

"No, sorry," said Justin. "We don't even know where they live."

Crane said, "Could you just explain something to me, then, Mr Hall? How do these things work? Is it just a case of whoever happens to be at the club on the night you'll hook up with?"

"Well, I suppose so." The flush was back.

"So the Cunningham's weren't exclusive partners. There were others that you both fucked."

After a stunned silence, Cynthia said, "Well, really!" There was no longer any sign of her neighing laugh, or horsey teeth. "There's no need to use that kind of language."

"Oh, so you don't mind having sex with strangers, you just don't like talking about it," said Crane as Anderson bent his head to his notes. But Crane could see the tell-tale upward tilt of the side of his mouth, meaning that Anderson was stifling a grin.

"I mean," she said sniffing, "that our private life is that just that. Private."

"Not when we are investigating the disappearance

and probable murder of Janey Carlton, it isn't."

The Halls groped for and found each other's hand.

"Murder?" Justin Hall said, his roving eye rolling to the left, before he managed to pull it back, so that both eyes focused on Crane.

"Yes, possible murder. Now, you have two options. One, you help us here and now by telling us what you know; or two, you refuse to speak and come with us to the nearest police station where you'll be cautioned for obstructing the course of justice." Crane had no idea if he and Anderson could do that, but it sounded good.

The couple looked at each other and it was Cynthia Hall that nodded at her husband and turning to Crane said, "What do you want to know?"

Letting out the breath he hadn't known he was holding, Crane smiled and said, "Tell me who Major and Mrs Cunningham were friendly with at the Mayfair Club." Crane felt he could moderate his language, now that they were co-operating.

"Well," Mrs Hall said. "We were thinking about this before you came. The man who paid Janey at lot of attention is called Zane. He comes to the club quite often, but always with a different, beautiful young woman. He would focus on the Cunninghams whenever they were there together. You should have seen his face if they went off with someone else."

"Who's face, this Zane's?" asked Anderson.

"Yes," nodded Justin. "He would get very angry if Janey and Clive chose a different couple and not him and his latest floosy. He flounced out a few times when that happened, but he was always back, he seemed to be drawn to Janey like a moth to the light."

"Do you know anything about him?"

"No," said Cynthia, "just his first name."

"Young, old, fat, thin?" said Anderson.

"Um, young, at least younger than us, so probably in his late 20's or early 30's, good body, good looking, dark shaggy hair, tall, I'd say over 6'," she said.

"Great description, thanks Mrs Cunningham," said Anderson. "I'd like to arrange for a colleague to come down and create a photo fit picture, if that's all right?"

"Of course," she said, nodding her agreement, as Crane and Anderson stood to leave. "And, um, you'll keep our names out of the media? Please?"

"We'll do our best. Thank you for your co-operation," said Anderson and he and Crane escaped out onto the street.

Crane rubbed his hand over his short dark hair. "This is turning into a surreal investigation, Derek."

"Don't I know it. It's certainly the strangest I've ever worked on," and after staring up at the house for a moment, he shoved his hands in his raincoat pocket and they both walked away.

"I'm not sure your raincoat gives quite the right impression here in Kensington, Derek," Crane said. "Are you sure you can't afford a new one?"

"You know very well I can, I just don't want a new one."

"Even though you look like a throwback to those clichéd TV detectives?"

"Yes, but think about it, people remember me, don't they?"

"That's true, but do they have any confidence in you?"

"Well, Columbo always got his man. So…"

"So?"

"So I rest my case."

Crane shook his head in disbelief and stopped to

light a cigarette. As Anderson waited for him, he asked Crane, "Where to now, do you think?"

"Well," Crane said after exhaling his first drag. "We've two options, either Major Cunningham, or the Mayfair Club. What do you think?"

"We're near to the Club," Anderson said.

"Good point," agreed Crane.

"On the other hand we could put this to the Major and get him to give us the details."

After a few contemplative puffs Crane said, "No. I want him in the dark as to the details of our investigations for the moment, so let's go back to the Mayfair Club and see the spiv Dante Skinner."

Twenty Two

"Oh, it's you, again," Dante said as he looked up when Crane and Anderson walked into his office. "What do you want this time?" Dante affected a bored look, but Crane wasn't taken in. The man was bouncing a pen up and down on his desk and seemed to have difficulty looking at them.

"Just a little more information, if you don't mind, sir," said Anderson.

"And if I do mind?"

"Let's not go there, eh?"

Dante put down his pen, "No, I suppose not."

Crane said, "We have been to talk to Mr and Mrs Hall, whose details you so kindly gave us. They told us of another customer who was quite taken by Janey Cunningham, but they only know him as Zane. Ring any bells?"

"Um…"

"Tall, good looking, dark shaggy hair, late 20's, early 30's," Anderson read from his notebook. "Tends to come in with a new woman every visit and seemed very, very taken by Janey Cunningham."

"To the point of obsession," added Crane.

"Exactly," agreed Anderson, "Any thoughts?"

In the silence that followed Anderson's question, Crane wandered around the office, if you could call it that, as it was more of a store room, and he noticed a stack of boxes against one wall. He walked over to them and started to open the top one.

"Hey," shouted Dante. "What do you think you're doing?"

"Nothing," said Crane over his shoulder, "Just looking around. Why? Have you something to hide?"

Dante pushed his chair backwards and stood up. "No, of course not, but I've not given you permission to search my premises."

Crane turned to face him. "What a good idea, Dante," he said smiling. "Thank you for that. Come on, Derek, if our friend Dante here isn't prepared to help us with the contact details of our mystery punter, then I'm sure a Judge will give us a search warrant, so we can find out the information for ourselves."

Anderson slowly nodded, "Good point, Crane. And who knows what else we might find whilst searching not just the office, but the whole place."

"Exactly," Crane agreed. "We could find drugs, firearms, details of clients paying for sex. You know," he said approaching the door, "I always thought there was something dodgy about this place. And now we'll be able to find out just what it is."

As Crane's hand reached for the door handle, Skinner shouted, "Stop!"

Crane let his hand rest on the handle and said, "Yes?"

"I think I know who you're talking about."

"You do?" Anderson said. "That's excellent."

Dante Skinner sat down heavily in his chair and

opened a drawer in his desk. Pulling out a file he flipped through it and then copied down some details onto a post it note. Handing it to Anderson he said, "Are we done now?"

"For now," he replied and Crane and Anderson smiled at Dante as they got ready to leave his office. "Until you see this Zane again, in which case you're to phone me," and Anderson flipped his card onto Dante's desk.

"I almost wish we had a warrant," Crane said once they'd closed Dante's office door. "He's definitely got extra-curricular activities going on here."

"I'm sure you're right, but at the moment finding Janey Cunningham is our top priority. Anyway, this is the Met's patch."

"Suppose so," said Crane reluctantly and followed Anderson up the stairs and out into the early evening sunshine.

Twenty Three

…His latest escort arrived right on time. Checking her out he saw honey blond hair, a beautifully tailored dress which showed that she had curves in all the right places and long legs that ended in stylish stilettos. She was as well groomed as any news presenter, television host, or actress. But perhaps those jobs didn't pay as much as her current one. £1,000 per night wasn't bad going, he supposed. A pretty good payday for her and easily affordable for him.

He had to admit that she was adorable, as they settled into the back seat of the car that he'd hired for the evening. Under the driver's steady hand, the car swept up the M3 and was soon depositing them outside the door of a restaurant in Farnham. Glamorous and attentive, she took his arm and whispered in his ear as they entered the restaurant and were shown to their table. She turned most of the male heads in the restaurant and he saw Major Cunningham do a double take when they walked past him. And why wouldn't he? For the escort could have been Janey's double. After delicious, yet dainty, French cuisine, which she hardly ate any of, they left the restaurant, the hired car and driver whisking them back to his house in London. Without a murmur she followed him into the house and accepted the balloon of brandy he handed her. They sat by the light of the fire and strategically placed candles, conversing quietly, until at last he rose, took her hand and led her to the bedroom.

Their lovemaking started out well enough. He enjoyed the silky softness of her skin, running his hands over her body, roaming, seeking and searching. Her firm breasts were perky, her legs long and agile. It was when he reared above her that it happened. An image of his mother came into his head. Filling him. Changing him. Beneath him, Janey Cunningham smiled seductively up at him, pouting her lips, her arms reaching for him. At first he relished her touch, gave himself up to the ministrations of his mother. Allowed her to make him feel wanted, attractive, alive in a way he hadn't before.

But as his climax began, his focus shifted once more. Beneath him was still Janey Cunningham, but now she was the whore who left him. The bitch who withdrew a mother's love before he'd even had time to experience it. The cow who had to pay for her abandonment of him. He wanted to wipe the smugness from her face. Watch her features contort into something horrible. Wipe away her good looks and expose her for who she really was. Expose the evil in her heart.

His hands went around his mother's neck. As he climaxed, he squeezed. His grip was as solid as a vice, rendering her struggles ineffectual. As she gasped for the air that was unable to pass through her closed throat and down into her lungs, her eyes bulged. She died with his name on her lips.

Replete, he rolled off her and sank into a dreamless sleep by her side.

The following morning he wrapped the body of his escort in a blanket, threw her over his shoulder and bundled her into the boot of his car. Driving to the nearby river, he tenderly laid her in the water and watched as her body sank down, coming to rest in the mud. Her limp limbs spread, tendrils of her hair framed her face and her dress billowed around her.

"Goodbye, mother," he whispered.

Twenty Four

Ninety six hours and counting and still no Janey Cunningham, no body, nor any ransom demand. It was proving difficult to locate the mysterious Zane, as it appeared that he had given false contact information to the Mayfair Club. When questioned on the telephone about this, all Dante had to say was that he was not a credit reference agency, nor a detective agency, and if a customer chose to give him false information, what was he supposed to do about it? Some people just went to great lengths to conceal their real identity and it was nothing to do with him. He'd fully co-operated with Crane and Anderson and didn't know what else he was supposed to do. The only concession they'd gotten out of Dante was that he would definitely phone them if Zane turned up at the club again.

And so Crane and Anderson had decided that it was looking less and less likely that Janey had been kidnapped, which put the spotlight firmly on the Major once again, hence the fact that he was currently sitting stewing in an interview room at Aldershot Police Station. After he'd been sitting there for half an hour on his own, Crane and Anderson joined him, sat at the table and Anderson put a large file down. The room was cold and austere and Crane's face matched the the room. He simply stared at Major Cunningham and didn't speak.

"Now look here, Crane, what's going on?" demanded the Major. He was on the verge of rising from his seat so Crane cut across him.

"I'm the one asking the questions, Major. So, to start with, what can you tell us about Zane Fisher?"

"Who?"

"Zane Fisher from the Mayfair Club. We understand you have had, shall we say, relations with him in the past."

"Never heard of him."

"Try again, sir," said Crane and repeated the description from Mr and Mrs Hall.

When Cunningham once more denied knowing him, Anderson rummaged in his file and slid over an artist's impression of the man in question. This time Cunningham couldn't hide the fact that Zane Fisher was known to him. His face began to look like a piece of tripe, white with darker dips and hollows in it. Was it fear or embarrassment? Crane was beginning to suspect there was more that Cunningham wasn't telling them. What was he hiding? What didn't he want them to know?

"Tell me about him," Crane said. "This Zane Fisher."

"He, he," the Major cleared his throat, "we met him at the Mayfair."

"And he was one of your liaisons?" Anderson asked.

"Yes."

"How often?"

"I suppose quite frequently, until…"

"Until what?" prompted Anderson.

"Until he became too pushy, too possessive, I suppose. Janey and I go, went, to the club for variety in our sex lives, not to get close to another couple. And he was beginning to give me the creeps."

"How so?" Crane asked keenly interested, his head tilting to one side as he listened to the Major's explanation.

"He would suddenly appear," said Cunningham. "You'd turn around and there he was. He was always watching us. Well, watching Janey I suppose. There was just something about him…" the Major thought for a moment. "It was as though there was something darker inside of him. Going to the Club was supposed to be for a bit of fun and he was definitely taking the fun out of it."

"So what did you do?"

"I suggested to Janey that we leave him alone. She thought it a shame because he was so attractive, but she did agree."

"So she liked this Zane?" said Anderson.

"Yes, I suppose so."

"And how did that make you feel?" Crane leaned over the table. When Cunningham didn't reply, Crane spoke for him. "Did it make you feel bad, inadequate, inferior and old? I bet your self-esteem fell through the floor didn't it?"

"I think it made you jealous," Anderson added to Crane's verbal bombardment. "Did it make you jealous enough to kill her?"

"No."

"Oh I think so, Major. Is that why you did it? So no one else could have her?"

"No."

"So you could keep her all to yourself?" said Crane.

"No! I haven't killed her!"

"Has she run away with him then?" the questioning was relentless. "Perhaps she preferred a younger model? Someone with a hard, muscular body, who wasn't going grey at the temples and slowing down?"

"What? What are you talking about?"

"If she has run away, its best you tell us now, sir," said Crane. "Before…"

"Before what?"

"Before we arrest you for murder."

"Murder? Arrest me? What are you talking about?"

"You're hiding things from us, Major. It's best you tell us now. Co-operate, or it could be the end of your army career," Crane said.

"NO! Shut up! I haven't done anything to her. I love her, she's my whole life, my wife, my love," and Cunningham broke down, covering his face with his hands, sobbing and blubbering about how he hadn't done anything to her, he couldn't kill her, he just couldn't.

Crane and Anderson left him alone then. Watching from the viewing room until the Major gradually regained control, Crane and Anderson then returned to the interview room and handed him a box of tissues and a bottle of water. Cunningham greedily glugged down half of the water and then wiped his face with a tissue.

"Perhaps you would be good enough to tell us the truth, now, Major Cunningham," Anderson asked.

Cunningham began slowly. "Janey had been moving further and further away from me lately. I don't know how much of that had to do with our lifestyle, or rather our sexual lifestyle," he wiped his nose. "But things weren't good between us. She liked to party. Hard. That involved lots of alcohol and she'd started taking drugs."

"Drugs?" Crane said.

"Yes, cocaine mostly, occasionally a few pills."

"And you?"

"No, I stayed clear of them. I can't take drugs, I'm in the army, I'm not that stupid, Crane. But she didn't like it. She accused me of not joining in. She said that my not wanting to experiment with new things made me boring and middle aged. We used to have such rows," Cunningham shook his head as he remembered. "Awful shouting matches," he sniffed and then took another drink of water. "But just because our marriage is going through a difficult patch doesn't mean I don't love her. I wanted it to work. I was trying my best to persuade her to slow down, to stay at home more."

"But she didn't want to?"

Cunningham shook his head. "I still love her now as much as I did on our wedding day. She is my heart, my life, my reason for getting up in the morning, my whole world. I just want her back," his voice began to break again. "I... just... want..." and then his sorrow overwhelmed him once more and he began to sob, slumping against the table, his head buried in his arms.

Crane and Anderson quietly removed themselves from the room, leaving him alone to grieve for his lost wife and his lost marriage.

Twenty Five

Crane and Anderson hadn't managed to get any more information out of Major Cunningham yesterday and so were sat by Crane's beloved white boards that morning, looking for inspiration.

"Any more luck with Zane Fisher?" asked Crane.

"Nope. As you know the address and phone number are fake."

"Has Dante Skinner been in touch?"

"Nope."

"Nothing more from Major Cunningham?"

"Nope."

"For fuck's sake," Crane slammed his hand down on the desk he was sitting by and then rose and started to prowl. "There must be something, something we've missed, something someone hasn't told us," he turned and gazed at his boards. "Right, let's start again," he decided.

"What?" Anderson was sat on an office chair, looking morose with his hands in the pocket of the raincoat he hadn't yet taken off.

"We must have missed something, so we need to start again. Review all the information we have.

Backgrounds, jobs, friends, family…"

Anderson got reluctantly off his chair and shook off his raincoat. "Oh very well, on one condition, well two actually."

"Let me guess," replied Crane, "A mug of tea and a piece of cake?"

"That's about right. If I'm going to expel lots of energy, I need a sugar boost to keep me going."

"So that's your excuse for your sweet tooth?"

"Yep and I'm sticking to it. Right, pass me over a folder, anyone will do, and I'll make a start."

Crane did as he was told and yelled for Sgt Williams to get the teas in, before grabbing a file himself. Crane wasn't necessarily a technophobe; it was just that the SIB liked to keep their paper files as well as having everything on computer. It was a throwback practice, and was kept as a concession when the SIB came under a voluntary review a few years earlier. They had a comprehensive computer system, including a search facility to look for similar crimes using keywords, but this time Crane wanted to review all the paperwork. His eyes seemed to glaze over when he spent too long at a computer monitor and he was afraid he might miss something important. Miss that one piece of vital information that seemed inconsequential, but could crack a case wide open. That was the buzz that kept Crane working as an investigator, a military police detective. He couldn't imagine doing anything else. As far as he was concerned it was a perfect combination of army life and policing. One wouldn't be the same without the other, they were like conjoined twins.

For a while, all that could be heard was the rustle of paper, slurp of tea and crunch of biscuits. Crane didn't even leave his desk for a cigarette, a sure sign of how invested he was in the case and how determined he was to find Janey Cunningham. He wasn't doing it for her husband, for he had very little sympathy or respect for Major Cunningham at that moment in time. The Cunningham's lifestyle was abhorrent to Crane. He simply couldn't imagine having sex with anyone other than his wife Tina. And the thought of Tina having sex with someone else and in front of him to boot, was so repulsive that the mere thought of it left a bad taste in his mouth.

After a while, the lure of nicotine became too strong for Crane to ignore, so he took the opportunity of clearing his head and having a wander outside. Not that there was much to see, just the Provost Barracks car park and the main thoroughfare through Aldershot Garrison. Every now and again a clutch of military vehicles rumbled past and soldiers came into view jogging around the playing fields. Crane took a deep breath. It was the smell that got to him every time. It was a bit like a layer cake. At the bottom was sweat and the middle layer was made up of male hormones. The top layer was a mix of engine oil and exhaust fumes and it was all topped off with a sprinkling of mud and grass. This was his home, where he felt most useful and most comfortable. Occasionally it was subtly suggested that Crane might be posted elsewhere, but he always resisted. Anyway the SIB at Aldershot covered the whole of Hampshire and the South East of England. The other large SIB contingent was based at Catterick and the North of England was too cold for him. So because of his experience in major crimes he'd managed to keep his post at Aldershot so far. But his reputation demanded that he solve this case and solve it quickly, so with renewed determination he ground out his cigarette and went back to his office.

Anderson was still hunched over a file, oblivious to everything, so Crane took a new one. Opening it, it contained the details of everything taken from Major and Mrs Cunningham's house, when the forensic teams had scoured through the dwelling looking for any sign that Mrs Cunningham had been murdered there, or abducted from there. Looking through the list of items, he found an entry for bank statements.

Bank statements were routinely taken in cases of missing persons. There could be anomalies in the accounts. Large payments made to unknown persons, perhaps the cost of having their partner, or child, killed or kidnapped. Horrible thoughts, but the police were paid to be suspicious. They couldn't afford to think that people of a certain social standing wouldn't break the law. The statements recovered from the house were in several names. A joint account for Major and Mrs Cunningham, an account in the name of Major Clive Cunningham, one in the name of Mrs Janey Cunningham and a fourth in the name of Janey Carlton. So there was one which was a joint account, but three accounts in individual names. Crane stilled. His skin began tingling, then his hands trembled, the paper he was holding fluttering slightly. He had spotted that there were a clutch of statements for a bank account in the name of Janey Carlton. Her professional account would appear to be separate from her personal account. He then checked and double checked the account numbers. Yes, it was clearly a different account. He looked at the evidence reference number given to the bank statements and on checking found they were stored at Aldershot Police Station in the evidence locker. Flicking through the pages in the file, he couldn't find photocopies of them.

"Derek," he called, keeping his voice light.

"Mmm,"

"Fancy a break?"

"What? Why?"

"Because I think I've found the missing link we've been looking for. We need to go to your place. Now."

Anderson's head snapped up at the words 'missing link' and clearly trusting his friend's instincts and not needing any further information, he grabbed his old raincoat and followed Crane out of the SIB office.

Twenty Six

Crane and Anderson, upon arrival at the police station, were quick to locate the bank statements they needed. They were rapidly photocopied, to give them one set each and after examining them, both men swiftly came to the same conclusion.

"Well?" asked Anderson.

"Well, we'll have difficulty getting anything out of her bank without a search warrant and that could take too long to come through."

"Agreed."

"The entries don't give us enough information."

"Agreed again," said Anderson.

"So?" asked Crane.

"So we go to see Laura Battle."

"Excellent, my thoughts exactly. Shall I drive?" and Crane grabbed his car keys.

During the car journey they tried not to speculate, Crane careful not to get carried away in his enthusiasm. Theories and wild guesses didn't really get an investigator very far. True, part of the job was intuition, found at the core of all good detectives. But good detectives also knew when to stay within the realms of possibility, not become carried away with fantasy.

Anderson had called Laura Battle as Crane drove, to ensure she stayed in her office. She'd grumbled a bit, but agreed to move a couple of appointments so that she could be available. Not that Anderson had left her any room for manoeuvre. He had been dogged in his demands that she stay put, the unspoken threat of arrest if she didn't, had been clear from the tone of his voice.

Upon their arrival, she let them into the building and they once more settled on the sofas.

"How can I help you this time, detectives?" she said, not sounding in the least bit happy at their sudden appearance.

Crane said, "We want to talk to you about Janey's expenditure."

"Pardon?"

"Her work expenditure. After all you're her agent, are you not? You must have a good idea of what's going on, how she's earning and spending her money and also know who her accountant is."

Laura had been fiddling with her cigarette packet, but stilled at Crane's words and took an involuntary intake of breath, her eyes widening in horror.

"Ah, I see you've an inkling of the information we want," he said to her.

Anderson said, "It seems clear from her professional bank account, the one in the name of Janey Carlton, that she paid a regular monthly payment of £2,000 pounds to what appears to be an estate agency."

The only parts of Laura Battle moving were her eye lids. She blinked them, rapidly.

"We need to know what that payment refers to, Ms Battle. Does Janey have a house or a flat in London that she rents?"

As her silence continued, Anderson told her, "If you don't co-operate to our satisfaction, we will easily get a search warrant for your premises, your computers and your company and private bank accounts, in order to find the information we require."

"This is vital, Laura," Crane said. "Janey could be there. Help us find her, please. Let's put an end to all of this."

"I had promised never to tell anyone," Laura Battle whispered looking anywhere but at the two men.

"If Janey is dead, it rather negates your promise doesn't it?" Anderson said.

"Do you think she's dead?"

Crane could hear the fright in her voice. "Laura," he said. "She's been missing for days now. There's been no ransom demand, so she wasn't kidnapped. She's not phoned anyone, so it's unlikely she's run away, for if that were the case, the desire to get in touch with at least you would be extremely strong."

"I take it you've not heard from her?" asked Anderson.

"No, no, I've not," she replied.

A tear had begun to track its way down Laura's make-up caked cheek, leaving a bright track mark in the foundation.

"So... the most likely scenario is that she's dead. Where is the property, Laura?"

Laura Battle got off the sofa and moved across to her computer, as if in a daze. She sat down, clicked a few keys, then pulled towards her a piece of paper and wrote on it. She then walked over to a cabinet on the wall and extracted a set of keys.

Anderson and Crane stood.

"Here's the address," she said and handed over the

keys and the note. "It's a flat, in London. It was private. Her sanctuary."

Crane swallowed his anger at the stupidity of the woman who had been withholding vital information, that could have save them a lot of time and trouble, and said, "And the income paid into that account and detailed on the statements, was that from her modelling assignments?"

Laura shook her head. "No. As I've already said, the modelling work was drying up because of her age. It's super hard to get jobs at the moment. She's at that difficult in-between age. Not young enough, but not yet old enough to be a mature model such as Twiggy."

"So where did the money come from? Where did she find another income stream from?"

Laura Battle sat down hard on the sofa. "She was a high class escort. Very high class," she whispered.

"She was a hooker," said Crane.

Laura Battle nodded, toppled over on the settee and sobbed.

Leaving the woman, as frankly Crane had no idea what to say to her, he and Anderson let themselves out of her office.

Once in the car Crane vented the anger he'd dared not let loose in the office. "Fucking bitch!" He smashed his hand down onto the steering wheel. "She could have given us this information three days ago! What is wrong with these people?"

"I don't know, Crane," Anderson said, sounding worn down rather than angry. "After all the years in this job, at times I still don't understand human nature. People cover up things for what they think are the best of reasons. They keep secrets when they should tell the truth and refuse to accept the reality that their loved one has been killed, or even is a killer."

"Will you arrest her for obstructing the course of justice?"

"Probably, but for now we need to get to London and get into this flat," and Anderson reached for his mobile.

"Who are you calling?"

"The Metropolitan Police. I've a bad feeling about this and I want them there when we open that door."

Twenty Seven

The sound of the opening music to 'Saturday Morning Kitchen' filled the air as Tyler walked into his own kitchen. Cooking was one of Penny's hobbies and she watched the program religiously every Saturday morning. Tyler, dressed in running gear, had grabbed the post off the mat at the front door as he'd passed and held the envelopes in his hand.

"Any coffee on?" he asked.

"Yes," said Penny grabbing a mug and pouring the hot, strong liquid into it. "You off for a run?"

"Umm, supposed to be, but, well, you know?" and he shrugged his shoulders. He took the mug from her, endured her laughter at his lack of commitment to his running regime and strolled out of the kitchen into their garden. It wasn't large, they were in London after all, but it was a beautiful, calm space, with a deck, a patch of grass and mature bushes and trees surrounding it. It was also a bit of a sun trap. He pulled a chair away from the wooden table on the decking and sat down, deciding to open his credit card statement first. It was cleared every month by direct debit from his bank account, but he liked to keep abreast of his expenditure.

It was a way of making sure he didn't become too frivolous. It was amazing how much brunch at Costa Coffee or lunch at Pret a Porter most days could add up and become a run-away expense.

The first thing he saw as he pulled the statement out of the envelope was the total. £5,000. The sum caused him some consternation. It wasn't that he couldn't cover it, but surely his spending wasn't that out of control? His normal bill was around £2,000 per month. There must have been some mistake. Perhaps a payment had had a full stop in the wrong place turning £24.75 into £247.50? Maybe a purchase for £100 had become £1,000 in error? Confident the balance could easily be explained away Tyler unfolded the paper and began to go through each item.

By the time he'd finished, he'd found that most of the statement was in order, but there were three payments that he couldn't explain. All were to some place called the Mayfair Club and were for £1,000 each. Tyler was still sat in his chair, drumming his fingers on the wooden table, when Penny came to join him.

"What a beautiful morning," she said, sitting down and lifting her face to the sun. "Don't you just love England in the sunshine?" she asked Tyler.

"Mmmm," he agreed vaguely, his mind elsewhere.

"I think I might take the girls to the park later. What about you? Decided what you're up to yet?"

"Oh, I think I'll go for that run after all," he said and he grabbed the post off the table, just managing to remember to kiss Penny as he left her. "See you later."

Tyler didn't really want a run it was just that he needed to get away from the house. He was beginning to feel like he was in a pressure cooker. His feelings of anger and confusion had turned to fear. His emotions were conspiring to make him feel trapped in a situation that he couldn't begin to understand and from which there was no way out.

As he jogged he tried to apply logic to the situation, in an attempt to work out what on earth was going on. First there had been the sexy underwear left on the bed. Then a single red rose on Penny's pillow. And now payments on his credit card that he didn't have a clue what they were for. Picking up his pace, he ran along the pavement and could feel the sweat building on his brow. But he could also feel drops of sweat popping open on his back as though his skin were on fire, and the sweat was trying to douse the blaze and failing. He stopped running, put his hands on his legs and panted. Looking up, he saw he was by a corner shop, and fumbling in his pocket for some change, he went in and purchased a bottle of water. He stood leaning against the outside of building as he emptied the half litre bottle.

He'd been putting it off, but now he had no choice but to make a decision and act on it. He must go to the police. Someone was messing with his life and he couldn't stand by any longer. He looked up and down the road seeing nothing more than a normal street in London, populated by people who were a colourful range of ethnicity. He used to feel safe in the streets around his home, but now he scanned the face of everyone who walked past him. But no one was paying him any attention that he could see. He turned his back on the people and stared at his reflection in the shop window. His hair was matted with sweat, his face red with exertion and fear and a muscle twitched in his thigh. He was just about to turn away and return home when he caught sight of a man reflected in the window.

He was dressed similarly to Tyler in a singlet and joggers, but he didn't seem sweaty or frightened, as Tyler was. He looked calm, his head slightly tilted on one side as he watched Tyler. A look of wry amusement crossed the man's features. Features that were identical to Tyler's own.

Tyler whirled around, focused on the point across the street where the man had been standing. But there was no one there. The man dressed in running gear, who had looked exactly like Tyler, had disappeared.

Twenty Eight

…It appeared his brother was doing well for himself. He had traced Tyler's life from school, to university, to work. It was once Tyler had started secondary school at the age of 11 that he had begun to show his potential. From information gleaned from the computer system of the prestigious school Tyler had attended, the boy had excelled at mathematics, just like his brother. However, instead of showing an interest in computers, he had leaned towards finance. A budding businessman, he'd joined the school's Small Business Club and learned all about product design, manufacture, sales and marketing. But according to written reports from his teachers, the London Stock Market was what had fascinated Tyler.

His A level examinations completed and passed with straight A's, his university education began at The London School of Economics. After graduating with a first class honours degree, Tyler had worked for a while as a stock market dealer, before joining a respected hedge fund firm. Once he'd settled-in there, it seemed Tyler had begun to show his flair for recruiting rich clients and then making them, and his firm, even richer. Tyler had profited as well, of course, resulting in his being a bit of a catch as a bachelor about town. It hadn't been long before he'd been snared by the lovely Penny.

As Tyler had continued his Midas-type meteoric rise in fortunes, he had done the same, but in a very much more subversive manner. Elusive and enigmatic, he'd emerged from his self-imposed exile like a butterfly from a chrysalis. The difference between the two brothers was not external, but very much internal. Tyler, a warm hearted family man was a world away from his darker, moody brother. Temperamental and inclined to crush those who got in his way, he looked just as beautiful as Tyler on the outside, whilst rarely showing those around him who he really was on the inside.

The only people who saw his sadistic, evil streak, were the girls who acted as his escorts. He was able to indulge his truly atrocious behaviours with those girls he paid handsomely to spend time with him. Every one of them had resembled his mother. Some had fought back and escaped into the darkness of the night and he'd never seen them again. No doubt they'd chalked the bad experience up to the dangers of their profession. Others, however, were not able to put up enough of a fight and were never seen again. By him, or by anyone else come to that.

Twenty Nine

Crane and Anderson were poised on the steps of a block of flats in Docklands. All sculpted concrete and metal, it looked like a flashy block for yuppie city types keen to show off their wealth. A video entry system was on the wall. They were going to Flat No 6, but there was no name against the button. Discretion assured, the absence of a nameplate seemed to say. Crane looked around the block as Anderson tried to find the right key for the communal entrance door. It was quiet to the point of bleakness. There were very few cars parked outside, testament to the underground car park for residents and the only sound was of faraway traffic, which filtered through the grounds towards them. This was clearly a private place for those not wishing to be observed or disturbed.

Anderson had by now found the correct key and they went through the entrance doors, followed by two detectives from the Metropolitan police. Anderson had refused to enter the apartment block until they had arrived. He insisted that procedure must be followed in order to protect the crime scene, if that was what they were about to be faced with. And he was very much afraid they were.

No one spoke as they walked up the stairs to the 2nd floor. There were two flats on the ground floor, three on the first and three on the second. Janey Cunningham's apartment was quiet. No sounds came through the front door and no one responded to Anderson's knock. Looking over at one of the Met detectives, who nodded his agreement, Anderson used the key to open the door.

As Crane walked into the apartment, the overwhelming first impression was the smell. The apartment seemed musty, abandoned and disused, but the underlying odour was of decay. The second impression was one of light. Crane was slightly taken aback by it as they walked from the dim communal hallway into a large open plan space. There was a bank of windows along one wall, leading out to a small balcony. The kitchen area was on their right and the lounge on their left. There was no sign of anyone. Nothing seemed to have disturbed the austerity of the place. Two shiny chrome and black leather settees stood arranged around a large television set which was mounted on one wall. In the middle of the space was a glass and chrome dining table with black chairs. By contrast the kitchen was white, with white marble work surfaces and white cupboards. There seemed to be nothing personal in the room at all and nothing out of place. They knew it was a one bedroomed flat, so Crane and Anderson went in search of the bathroom and bedroom, whilst the two men from the Metropolitan police looked through the lounge and kitchen.

Crane found the bathroom. The austere theme carried on throughout the apartment. In the bathroom black wall tiles offset chrome and white fittings. There was a large shower stall and separate bath. Crane looked into the bath, but it was gleamingly clean and completely dry. He moved to the shower stall. It was built into a corner and the two glass walls were frosted. Crane wondered what secrets could be hidden behind them and moved to open the glass door. His hand was reaching for the handle when Anderson called to him.

"Crane! In here."

Crane ran the few paces to the bedroom door and peered over his friend's shoulder. Anderson had found Janey Carlton in her bedroom.

Crane wished they could have found her sleeping, ill in bed, or enjoying a lie in. Anything but the sight, and smell, that greeted them. The black satin sheets on the large bed were in disarray, with stains on them that could have been body fluids or blood. It was difficult to discern which on the dark sheets. Cushions were scattered around the floor, discarded in either passion or anger. Women's clothing was draped across a chair set in front of a large dressing table. A mirror was placed on the wall above it. Reflected in the glass Crane could see Anderson, who was standing at the foot of the bed. He could also see two naked feet on the floor down by the side of the bed.

It was some while before they were able to take a better look at the body. They'd immediately left the bedroom and a call had been made urgently requesting a police forensic team. Once the specialists had arrived and everyone was suited and booted, Crane and Anderson were allowed back into the bedroom for a visual inspection only. They were not allowed to touch or move the body under any circumstances.

Janey Cunningham was lying on her back on the floor, lodged between the bed and the wall. Her skin was pale, punctured by bruises, with black and yellow marks that were visible on her wrists and ankles, although they were no longer bound. Blood matted her hair on one side of her head and from Crane's vantage point he could see bits of what appeared to be bone in and around the exposed wound. Her eyes were open and already clouded by death. One hand was covered in blood. Written in blood on the magnolia painted wall next to her, was a single word. Zane.

Thirty

Janey Cunningham's dead body had raised more questions than answers, which Crane and Anderson debated as they left the apartment and stood in the weak sunshine outside the block of flats. The press hadn't got wind of their grizzly find yet, so they were undisturbed, apart from the police constables guarding the entrance and the forensic personnel walking backwards and forwards, taking in supplies and taking out evidence.

"She clearly died from blunt force trauma," said Anderson. "They might find the murder weapon in the flat."

"Not that there's much there in the way of ornaments, or furniture come to that."

"Well, it was clearly a workplace, not a home."

Crane agreed with a small smile. "She seemed bruised all over, not just where her feet and wrists were bound."

"Mmm," agreed Anderson. "Very rough sex?"

"If so, she didn't pick her client very well, did she? It looks like she managed to snag a psychopath instead of a rich business man."

"So, was she meeting a client? Was it a liaison that went wrong? Or was it a deliberate murder, her death being the objective, not sex?"

"That's the question isn't it?" Crane scratched the scar under his beard.

"And the word Zane?" asked Anderson.

After a moment Crane said, "Well, there could be a couple of scenarios. Zane killed her and she managed to write his name before she died. Or Zane killed her and he wrote his name as a signature, claiming the kill." That last thought made Crane go cold.

"Or maybe it wasn't Zane who killed her and she was calling for Zane to help her?" Anderson suggested.

"If she wanted help, why not write her husband's name? But then again, they weren't getting on too well according to the Major." Crane said and lit a cigarette, before he continued speaking. "What's with the bruises looking as though she were bound hand and foot? But when we found her there were no restraints."

"Left for dead?"

"Eh?" asked Crane.

"She could have been tied up whilst the maniac tortured and then killed her. He took the restraints with him and left her for dead. She then regained consciousness, rolled off the bed and wrote the name on the wall before she died."

"Poor cow," said Crane. "No one deserves to die like that, whatever their profession. Being a prostitute, albeit a very expensive and exclusive one doesn't mean that she could be discarded like a piece of rubbish. She was a human being with hopes and dreams and desires, just like everyone else."

Their conversation was interrupted by one of the Met detectives, Detective Constable Saunders. "Sir," he addressed Anderson, "We've found what seems to be an address book. It looks like it's her client list. It was hidden in the bathroom, behind the panel covering the side of the bath.

"Good find," said Anderson.

"Thank you, sir. The chief investigating officer said to tell you that we'll have a copy for you later today, you can pick it up from New Scotland Yard if you like."

"Much appreciated," said Anderson and he turned to Crane. "While we're waiting, let's go and see Major Cunningham. He said he'd be at the London house." Turning back to the policeman, he said. "We'll break the news to the Major of his wife's death. As we've been investigating her disappearance and he knows us."

"Very well," the detective said. "See you later at the Yard, sir," and he hurried back into the building.

"Shall we?" Crane said, holding up his car keys and Anderson nodded his agreement.

Neither man was very enthusiastic about the task they were about to perform, having to tell a husband that his wife's body had been found. But the Major and his father deserved to hear the news as soon as possible and from policemen that they knew.

As Crane drove, he mulled over the many times he'd had to report the death of a loved one. A young army wife dying because the military spirited a killer away, which allowed him to kill again many years later; young girls raped and killed by a soldier (definitely one of Crane's lowest points); telling a girl her best friend had been killed by a punter. And now he had to tell an army Major that his wife was not only a high class hooker, but was dead. The job never got any easier.

They were shown into the drawing room of the house in Notting Hill by the same staid butler. Major

Cunningham rose at their entry. He took a step towards them, mouth open as though to ask them what the hell they wanted this time. But he closed it when he saw the expression on Crane and Anderson's faces.

"You've found her," he whispered. "She's dead?" At Crane's nod he groped behind him for the settee and sat down heavily.

"We're very sorry for your loss," intoned Anderson.

"Where is she?" Lord Garford asked. He was still standing, but every muscle in his body seemed tensed, as though he were readying himself for worse news to come.

"At a flat in Docklands," said Crane.

"A flat? Docklands? What the hell?" Major Cunningham stood up once again.

"Please sit down, sir," said Anderson. "We'll talk you through what happened. Tell you what we know at the moment."

Crane and Anderson had already agreed in the car exactly how much information they would give Janey's husband. They were going to stick to the known facts and leave out their speculations and some details of the manner of her death.

Anderson said, "We found out from Janey's agent, Laura Battle, that Janey rented a property in Docklands."

"Why would she need a flat we didn't know about?" asked Lord Garford.

"We understand that she entertained there."

"Oh, God," groaned the Major.

Crane and Anderson looked at each other as Major Cunningham began to weep. Anderson turned to Lord Garford, "Perhaps some tea, sir?"

"Something stronger I think," he said and he walked

across to a small table where a cut glass decanter and an array of small tumblers stood. He poured a large measure of something into one of the glasses and took it over to Major Cunningham.

He put his hand on his son's shoulder then said, "Here, Clive, drink this." As the Major looked up he continued, "Come on, lad, take it. Its brandy. For the shock."

Major Cunningham nodded and with a shaking hand managed to get the glass up to meet his lips. They all waited as he drank.

When the Major had drunk enough brandy and managed to sit back on the settee, still holding the class in two hands, Lord Garford asked, "How did she die?"

"At the moment we suspect it was blunt force trauma to the head, sir. They haven't found the murder weapon yet."

At the word 'murder' Clive Cunningham started to cry again. Then moan. His face distorted into a grimace as he realised he had to face life without his wife. He began to call her name over and over.

There was little any of them could do to comfort him and they all stood around not knowing quite what to do next in the face of such raw emotion from the Major. Crane was feeling rather awkward and imagined the other two men were as well, so he tilted his head in the direction of the door and said, "Shall we?"

The three men congregated in the hall. "Sorry, sir," said Crane. "I'm not deliberately being insensitive to the Major's grief, but if we could give you the information we have, then we can leave to carry on with our investigation. A family liaison officer is on his way," Crane looked at Anderson who nodded his agreement.

"Thank you," said Lord Garford. "I'm not sure one

is necessary, though. I can look after Clive."

"Of course," said Anderson, "it's merely procedure, sir. He or she can act as a liaison between the police and the family. Keep you up to date with the investigation, relay any questions you may have and such like."

"Very well," his Lordship agreed. "So what else do you know at the moment?"

"We've found a little black book," said Anderson. Lord Garford raised his eyebrows. "I mean literally a little black book. We think it contains details of her, shall we say, clients and so we'll be following that up."

"Dear God, she really was a hooker then." Lord Garford rubbed his hands over his face and then through his hair.

When he looked back at them, Crane said to him, "It would appear so, sir. We're going to concentrate on her client list. It could be that one of them…"

"I understand," Lord Garford said. "We didn't really know her at all, did we? Clive thought her absences meant that she was away modelling, but it seems not."

"No. According to Laura Battle, it appears the modelling had all but dried up, so she turned to another profession to make money."

"But why would she need money? She and Clive were pretty well off from what I know of their finances."

"I think it was more a matter of pride," said Anderson. "She didn't want Clive to know she could no longer command large five figure sums for a few photos. That and maybe greed."

"Or a need for independence," commented Crane. "Her own money gave her that."

"But surely she didn't need independence? Why wouldn't she let Clive support her? And of course, they'd inherit this in due course. I don't think I'll ever understand women," said Lord Garford.

"Amen to that," agreed Crane

Thirty One

Crane and Anderson had just left the house in Notting Hill when Anderson got a call. After several nods, 'yeses' and a 'copy that' Anderson killed the call.

"Copy that?" said Crane. "You've been hanging around the military far too long, Derek," and he laughed.

"I mustn't forget, 'Roger, over and out'," grinned Anderson.

"Do you copy?"

"Affirmative," laughed Anderson and the two men enjoyed a few light hearted moments after the brutal murder scene and the stress of having to tell the family that Janey was dead. Should Lord Garford or Major Cunningham have seen them, they would have been horrified by their display of levity, but it was a necessity for the two men. It helped to dispel the awful image of Janey Cunningham lying dead in her flat and the sounds of a man being broken by the news of his wife's death.

As Crane combatted the London traffic Anderson said, "What do you think of the Major now? Is he a suspect?"

"I don't think it's him," replied Crane. "He was too

badly affected by the news."

"Could it have been a display of emotion for our benefit?"

"No, I don't think so, Derek. Don't forget the Major is a soldier and soldiers don't really do emotion. We have to lock our feelings up in a box and throw away the key. The last thing you want to do after coming back from a tour is to cry all over your wife. Or cry all over your mates come to that. And it is worse for an officer. They take 'stiff upper lip' to a new dimension."

"So strike the Major?"

"I'd say so. It's far more likely a client. Was that what that phone call was about?"

"Yes, our Janey was a bit sneaky it seems. The Met found a hidden camera in a smoke detector on the ceiling of the bedroom. Her laptop is full of images of clients. Men and women."

It was a good job Crane had to concentrate on driving, but his surprise at Anderson's statement still washed over him, as though he'd had a load of cold water launched at him during a water bucket challenge. Crane took his eyes off the road for a moment and glanced at Anderson.

"Women?"

"Yep."

"Bloody hell," said Crane and turned his attention back to the road.

"They've started analysing the images already, so there may be some news for us when we get there."

"If we ever do get there in this bloody traffic," said Crane, leaning on the car horn as yet again someone cut him up. "This is why I don't drive in town. The underground is much better."

"Oh, so you prefer being a subterranean sardine in a

tin rather than up here in the light riding on the dodgems."

"You've got that right," said Crane, accelerating to do some cutting up of his own as he swerved into the outside lane on the dual carriageway. He was glad he'd done an Advanced Driver Training course, the amount of defensive and offensive manoeuvres he'd had to make. He was trying hard to concentrate on the traffic as he approached the Hyde Park Corner roundabout, but Anderson seemed oblivious to Crane's focus on the traffic and continued chatting about the case.

"Was she trying to blackmail her client's do you think?"

"Maybe, maybe not," Crane said braking sharply as the traffic in front of him suddenly stopped. Once their car was stationary, Crane turned to Anderson. "If she was charging a lot of money for her services, which she was according to Laura Battle, then I think the video was more for insurance. For a rainy day, if you like."

"Ah, so she could blackmail someone in the future if she needed a bit of a cash injection."

"Yes. I think she would have been calculating enough to do that, she certainly had a business like attitude."

The car was moving again, when Anderson suddenly shouted, "Bloody hell!"

"What? What?" cried Crane thinking they were about to have an accident and he looked frantically around him.

"Maybe her murder is on video!"

Anderson's credentials give them access to the car park at New Scotland Yard and they paced around the foyer until someone came to collect them.

It was DC John Saunders, whom they'd met at the

crime scene. He was a tall young man, with severely short hair which emphasised his large ears. He was dressed in a muted suit, shirt and tie. Around his neck hung his security pass.

"What's on the video clips?" Anderson asked Saunders, but didn't get a reply as they followed the policeman through the maze of floors and corridors. Eventually they arrived at the right office and saw the other detectives who had been with them at the crime scene. Saunders told them that it had been agreed he could give them a copy of Janey's little black book and also show them to an office where they could review the video clips taken from her computer.

As they sat down and Saunders opened the correct file for them on a laptop, Anderson asked his question again. "What's on the clips? Does it show her murder?"

"No such luck, sir," Saunders said. "It seems she turned the camera on when she wanted it to run. Here look," and he ran the first clip.

Crane and Anderson watched as the video started. Janey could be seen walking away from a dressing table, towards the bed, where a naked man was lounging. The view of her back showed she was dressed in something black, lacy and sheer.

Saunders continued, "The search of the flat revealed the remote 'record' button on the back of the dressing table, just by the corner, within easy reach of her fingers. We had a quick flick through and all of them start with her walking into view from the direction of the dressing table."

"Oh well," Anderson sighed. "I should have known it wouldn't be that easy."

"Come on then, Columbo," Crane said. "Take off your mac and let's get going. You take the computer and I'll take the book."

"Not a chance," said Anderson. "I'm more likely to delete the clips when trying to view them. I'll take the book," and Anderson swiftly swiped it off the table. "Let's just say it's your punishment for calling me Columbo."

Crane grinned and swapped seats with Anderson. Taking off his suit jacket, he rolled up his white shirt sleeves and loosened his tie ready to get on with the job. It wasn't something he was looking forward to, seeing the victim naked, having sex with numerous men and women, but it was one of those awful jobs he just had to get on with. He turned to his jacket and took his notebook out of the inside pocket. "I'll make a note of the names of the men as I go along," he said to Anderson. "Then we can correlate them with the book. She must speak to them and call them by their names at some point."

"Mmm, okay," said Anderson, already immersed in the photocopied pages of Janey's book.

As Crane clicked on the first file, he knew it was only the beginning of this part of the investigation. All those on the videos would have to be identified and contacted to see if they had an alibi for the approximate time of Janey's murder. At least all the work wouldn't fall to Crane and Anderson. It was more a case of them helping the Met, not the other way around. Janey Cunningham had been killed on their patch. It was just the way it worked. Still putting off his task, Crane then phoned Tina to tell her he'd be home late, yet again. Then, having run out of excuses, he clicked open the first video file and began.

Thirty Two

Crane had to confess to being impressed by the speed of the Met's investigation. With a lot of manpower at their disposal, they'd managed to identify many of Janey Cunningham's clients through correlation between her address book and the videos and were in the process of contacting them. For the moment it seemed everyone was more or less in the clear. Alibis had been sought for the approximate time of her death and were in the process of being verified. Crane thought back to his own office and the amount of work that normally he and Sgt Billy Williams had to plough through on their own, making him wistful for a larger team. But with the recent purges, which involved cutting back the manpower in the British Army, it was a futile wish. Most of the time he was just thankful he still had a job.

Crane stood and stretched, needing to ease the knots in his spine from reviewing his section of the video clips. He wondered how many of the policemen and women doing the same thing were being put off sex from reviewing a surfeit of sexual encounters, many of which had some kinky aspect or other to them. They had found a cupboard full of sex aids in the flat and it was clear Janey and her clients had put them to good use. She seemed to have been as professional as a hooker, as she had been as a model. He was just considering going out for a cigarette when DC Saunders called for him and Anderson.

They walked over to his desk, Anderson slightly behind Crane, scurrying to keep up.

"Have you got something?" Crane asked, hopeful of a distraction from his current task.

"Something that might help shed some light on the case, but we don't think he's the murderer. It's a man, who started out as a client, but says their relationship developed to the point that they became a couple."

Crane couldn't imagine having a relationship with someone who worked as a prostitute, but he kept his opinion to himself.

"If you're up for it, the boss has said we can go and interview him."

"Now?"

Saunders nodded. "Now. Are you coming?"

"Bloody right we are," said Anderson and to Crane's amusement Anderson rushed back to their cubbyhole office for his mac, as God forbid he should lose it. By now it was early evening, so they agreed that Anderson and Crane would follow DC Saunders in their own car and would then go home after the interview. The man they were going to interview luckily lived in West London, so it should be a fairly easy run home afterwards.

Andrew Ferris lived in a large house in the leafy suburb of SW19, made famous by the lawn tennis championships held there every year at the Lawn Tennis Club. It was an affluent, upmarket area, with large detached houses no doubt worth many millions of pounds. As they drove around the area, Crane wondered which house belonged to Andy Murray, the tennis player who was currently the World No 3 and a source of much British pride.

They swept into the driveway of Ferris' house and he opened the door to greet them. Once the introductions had been made and Ferris led them through to the kitchen, Crane had a chance to appraise the man they'd come to see. As they sat down around a huge wooden kitchen table a large, shaggy, grey dog padded over to them and sunk down on the floor next to his master. With his head on his paws, the dog surveyed the men, looking up with eyes that swivelled from one man to the other, causing his eyebrows to raise in turn. Crane smiled at the dog's unconscious cuteness and then looked at his owner.

Sometimes owners look like their dogs and it was certainly the case here. Ferris had large grey speckled bushy eyebrows which he had a habit of wiggling and whiskers sprouted out of his ears. In his 60's and not unattractive, he had an air of casualness about him. He seemed to be a man who knew himself well and was comfortable in his own skin. His clothes were casual, polo shirt and slacks, but clearly very expensive. Crane fancied the polo logo on his shirt was the real deal, not a cheap knock-off. He wore leather loafers with tassels and the shoes gleamed in the overhead spotlights as Ferris sat sideways in his chair at the table, one leg crossed over the other.

"We understand you knew Janey Cunningham. In fact you knew her rather well," said DC Saunders, his notebook open and pen poised to record the man's answers.

"Yes, that's correct," he told Saunders, with a tinge

of embarrassment on his cheeks. "Look, first off I want to say I'm sorry. I really must apologise for not getting in touch with you lot sooner."

"We'll get to that later," admonished Saunders. "For now can you tell us how you two met?"

"Oh, I was a client of hers," Ferris said. "I'm a widower and well, I was quite a successful business man before I retired early and therefore of independent means, so women tended to only want to know me for my money. I wasn't into that type, so I found it preferable to pay for an escort than bother with the money grabbing divorcee set. I answered Janey's advert on a discreet website."

"Which was?" Saunders asked.

"Oh, um, Park Lane Escorts. She went by the name Annabelle. You then clicked through to her personal website and made an appointment on line."

"Paying by?"

"Credit card."

"Did you know who she was then? Did you know that she was the model Janey Carlton?"

"I knew there was a strong resemblance. When I asked her she denied it, saying she just looked like her that was all and joked about Janey Carlton not needing to indulge in her type of work. It wasn't until we, well, became closer, that she confessed who she really was, but she swore me to secrecy."

"What did she tell you?"

"She told me all about her life. She confessed that she was unhappy in her marriage and that she had become an escort because there was no modelling work for someone of her age. She was struggling with both money and self-esteem. I found her to be rather vulnerable, which is what drew me to her in the first place, I suppose."

"You wanted to take care of her?" Crane heard the scepticism in Saunders' voice.

"Yes, I believe so, at least initially. It was later that the relationship became more balanced. As we saw more of each other, I began to appreciate her inner strength. She may have been fading as a model, but she was rising as an escort. She was determined to do whatever it took."

"To do what?"

"To become financially independent. She wanted out of the marriage but was realistic enough to understand that she had to do it on her own terms. She said her husband's wealth was tied up in the family estate so she wouldn't get anything much in a divorce settlement. Her father in law had even bought them the house in Farnham, so there would be no proceeds for her from the sale of that."

"So what happened, Mr Ferris? The last time you saw her?"

"It was several nights ago. We'd agreed that she was going to leave her husband for me. I'd asked her to marry me and she'd finally said yes." Ferris' eyes filled with tears. Dashing them away he carried on. "She was supposed to tell her husband that night that she was leaving him. It was all pre-arranged. I was waiting around the corner with the car. She came running towards me, clambered into the car, said it was done and off we went."

"What about the shoe?" asked Crane.

Ferris smiled at the memory. "She'd changed into flat shoes after he'd left to go back to the restaurant for his wallet, but had crammed the stilettos in her handbag. She hadn't wanted to leave them behind.

Manolo Blahnik's or some such they were. Anyway, one must have fallen out of her bag. We didn't realise until we got to her flat and by then it was far too late to go back."

"And what was your plan from then on?"

"I dropped her at her apartment. She was going to meet me at the airport the next evening. I'd booked us flights and we were going to my villa in Portugal. She said she had one last client, a booking that she couldn't cancel. She'd told everyone else she was retiring, all her regular clients that was, and after that one last booking, she was done with it all."

"So what did you do?"

"I tried to persuade her to change her mind, of course, tried to get her to cancel, but she wasn't having any of it. A job was a job, she said and she wanted to leave with everything straight. Finished. A clean break." Once again Ferris paused and wiped his eyes. "So I left her and I went home. By then it was the early hours of the morning, I'm not sure of the time. The following day I bumbled about packing, notifying my staff of my movements, and making sure that all was ready at the villa in Portugal. I left for the airport around 5pm. We'd arranged to meet there at 6 o'clock."

"But she didn't show?" asked Saunders.

Ferris could only shake his head. He was choked with emotion and appeared to have difficulty breathing. Crane moved into the kitchen, grabbed a glass off the counter and filled it with water. He handed it to Ferris who nodded his thanks and sipped at it for moment before clearing his throat and continuing with his story. "I waited until long after the flight had departed. I rang and rang her mobile, but there was never any answer. When I left the airport, I went to her flat, but there was no reply to my buzzing. I was crushed. I thought she'd changed her mind. I felt like such an old fool. I was so embarrassed. I shut myself up in this house, feeling sorry for myself, only going outside to walk the dog."

"Didn't you see the television news? Realise that she was missing?"

By now Ferris was once again crying. "Like I said I thought she'd taken me for an old fool and gone off with someone else. And then, then," he sniffed, taking deep breaths, his voice shaking with emotion, "You lot rang and told me that she had been found. Murdered. In her flat." He stood. "I'm sorry, excuse me," and he tripped and stumbled out of the room.

No one spoke as they waited for Ferris to return, which he did, with red eyes, his hands and the front of his polo shirt, damp. "To think I doubted her," he continued as though he'd never left the room. "That's the worst of it. She would have come with me. Married me. Now I know that she would. But someone killed her. So she couldn't. Such a tragic waste of life."

Crane wasn't altogether too sure if he was talking about Janey's life or his own future life. "You didn't have a key to her apartment?" he asked.

Ferris shook his head. "No, there was never any need. She didn't live there, not really. It was only a place for business. If only I had…." His voice trailed off.

DC Saunders looked at Crane and then Anderson who both nodded their agreement to his unspoken suggestion that they leave. "Thank you for being so frank, Mr Ferris," Saunders said. "Perhaps you could come to New Scotland Yard to make a formal statement tomorrow. Someone will be in touch to arrange it and we'll send a car for you."

"Of course," Ferris said and looked down at the dog

and began stroking his head. He was clearly lost in his memories and turning to his canine companion for solace, so the three men let themselves out of the house.

At the cars, Crane said, "If we're all agreed Ferris didn't murder her…" The other two murmured their agreement. "Then we need to find out who that last client of hers was."

Thirty Three

Tyler had decided to start his investigations with the credit card company. Then, armed with that information, he'd go to the police. Making a decision had made him feel better, but for some reason he couldn't still the looming sense of dread he kept experiencing. Something was definitely not right, but the trouble was he didn't know what it was. He'd kept putting off going to the police, or ringing the credit card company, as though by not acknowledging anything was happening, it would make it all go away. Not like him at all.

Determined to finally do something about it, and sat in his office, cocooned by the familiar noises of telephones ringing, people talking and moving around, he picked up the handset of his own telephone and called the customer service number on his credit card statement. He heard the muffled sound of the call ringing at the other end of the line and then a robotic voice welcomed him to the company and requested that he listen to the following list, and dial the number corresponding to his type of request.

He pressed the number one for bill query and had to

endure the awful music that all large companies seemed to use, to delineate the holding pattern that his call was in. As he tapped his pen on the desk in frustration, he began to feel like a large aircraft being forced to circle an airport high in the skies, waiting for the gap that would allow it access to terra firma.

"Thank you for your call," a voice said.

Tyler quickly interjected, "I'm calling to query my - "

But his sentence was cut short as he realised he was still pacing the fringes of the lion's den that was customer services. "Please continue to hold. A representative will be with you shortly."

Tyler continued to simultaneously tap his pen, listen to the music and watch the stock market. Glancing at the clock on his computer he realised he had been holding for 10 minutes already. All he wanted to do was to tell them that the three £1,000 charges to the Mayfair Club were nothing to do with him. What could be simpler or, more to the point, quicker?

After 15 minutes he was clenching his fists and could feel his blood pressure rising. The thump, thump, thump of his pulse started to reverberate in his ears. He was fortunate the markets were steady, or he would have been forced to kill the call.

The voice saying, "Good morning, this is Cherry speaking, how may I help you?" actually took him by surprise, as in his mind he was exploring possible explanations for the inexplicable doppelganger he had seen in the shop window a few days earlier.

"Oh, right," he managed and started to tell the girl of his problem.

"For security reasons please key in the number of your credit card on your handset now," she said.

"Can't I just give it to you?"

"No, for security reasons, please key in the number of your credit card on your handset now," she repeated and the line went dead.

Tyler took the telephone away from his ear and looked at it. Was anyone still there? He had no idea, but supposed he should do as the girl asked, so he keyed in the long number on his telephone keypad. Putting the receiver back to his ear, he heard a few clicks and whirrs and then the girl miraculously returned.

"Thank you," she said. "Can I have your name please?"

Tyler obliged and then said, "There are items on my statement I don't understand."

"Your date of birth?" the girl asked, ignoring Tyler's earlier words.

"Very well," he sighed and gave her the date.

"Please give me the answer to your security question."

Tyler exploded, "Look, I've been waiting 15 minutes and all I want to do is to explain…"

"Please give me the answer to your security question," the girl repeated, not at all flustered by Tyler's interjection. "What is the name of your family pet?"

"For God's sake, we don't have a family pet!"

"Thank you, that is the correct answer," Cherry was beginning to sound robotic and was clearly sticking to her script. "How may I help you?"

"I've been trying to tell you that there are three items on my statement that I don't know anything about."

"What is the date of the statement you are referring to?"

At Tyler's answer she said, "Thank you, I have that

information on my screen. Could you identify the payments in question?"

"The three payments to the Mayfair Club for £1,000 each."

"I can see those, please hold."

"But, wait," spluttered Tyler, but it was no good, she'd gone and he was once more subjected to the music. He timed her. It took three minutes and 30 seconds before she returned.

"Those payments seem to be in order, sir."

"In order? What on earth do you mean? How can they be in order? I didn't make the payments."

"The correct number, name, expiry date and security code was given for each transaction."

"But that's impossible! I didn't make them! I've never been to the Mayfair Club!"

"You don't need to have been. It was a 'no physical card transaction'."

"What on earth does that mean?"

"It means the transaction was made either by phone or over the internet."

"But I didn't authorise them!"

"Is there anything else I can help you with you today?" asked Cherry.

"What? No! I - "

But once again he was interrupted. "Thank you for calling and I hope you have a nice day."

With that Cherry was gone, leaving Tyler fuming. He banged his fist down on the desk, pushed back his chair and hurried to the men's room. As he paced the tiled floor he couldn't believe the indifferent attitude of the girl. How dare she dismiss his complaint just like that and then put the phone down on him! He was a good customer, damn it. He had a good mind to complain.

He caught sight of himself in the mirror. His shirt was stained with sweat, his hair in disarray where he'd continually run his hand through it and his face flushed. Where was the cool, calm, hedge-fund manager? Where had he gone? Tyler looked down and saw his hands were trembling.

Turning on the cold tap at a nearby sink, he scooped up water in his hands and bathed his face, rubbing the cool water across the back of his neck. He had to get a handle on his fear, as it was fuelling his anger. It was causing the trembling limbs and the lack of any control over his emotions. He wiped his face and took several deep breaths, before leaving the toilets, determined to call the police, just as soon as he had time.

Thirty Four

Crane decided to bring his boss up to date on the Cunningham case in Draper's office, rather than at the white boards downstairs, having something of a somewhat sensitive nature to tell his boss.

"Ah, Tom," Draper said at Crane's arrival. "I hear you've something for me."

"Yes, boss," said Crane and sat at Draper's signal. "The Met have been as good as their word and rushed through the autopsy on Janey Cunningham. I've a copy for you here."

"Thanks," said Draper as he took the paper file from Crane's outstretched hand. He didn't open it, but said, "Give me the salient points, please."

"Yes, sir," replied Crane and flipping open his own copy of the report said, "The Home Office pathologist has confirmed the cause of death was blunt force trauma to the side of her head. She had been bound hand and foot at some point, indicated by the abrasions found there. But in addition, her body had been subjected to a bad beating. There were no defensive wounds, such as on the side of her arms, which there would have been if she'd tried to protect her head and face with them, from which the pathologist surmises that she was still tied up during the attack. It seems it was frenzied and some sort of cosh was used. But they have been unable to identify the murder weapon as yet. There was also damage to her internal organs and bleeding from the spleen. He estimates the number of blows could be as high as 30, although it was difficult to tell because of multiple blows to the same part of the body. She had also been repeatedly, partially strangled."

"Come again?"

"The pathologist thinks it was some sort of erotic game. The killer kept strangling her as they had sex, but always stopped before she died."

"And he knows that how?"

"Because there was repeated bruising from hands and fingers on her neck, all in slightly different places, and damage to her trachea."

Crane fell silent as Captain Draper briefly closed his eyes.

When his boss opened them again, Crane continued speaking. "The pathologist thinks she may have been subdued with some sort of drug so she was pliable enough to tie her up, but if that was the case, anything she might have taken would have metabolised by now and no longer be in her bloodstream. Alternatively, she could have been frightened into submission with say a knife or a gun, although no such weapon has been found."

Draper nodded and Crane cleared his throat before continuing. "She had had rough sexual intercourse, as indicated by the tearing and bruising of that part of her body. Her partner hadn't used a condom therefore they have semen for analysis."

"Any news on that analysis yet?"

It was Crane's turn to close his eyes as he said, "It is a familial match to Janey Cunningham."

"What?" Draper sat upright. "Father, brother, what?"

"Child, we think," said Crane. "That was the other thing the autopsy found. She'd had a child that no one seems to have known about. Ergo, she'd had sex with her own son."

"Jesus Christ! How the hell am I supposed to tell Major Cunningham that?"

Crane had no idea, but was very glad Draper had said he was going to tell him. Crane hadn't wanted that job for all the tea in China.

"Anderson and I thought we'd go and see Janey's mother again," Crane said. "See if we can get anything out of her about her daughter having a son."

"Good idea," said Draper. "Maybe I should wait until you've seen her. Then at least I might have more information to take to the Major, rather than just that shocking piece of news. Off you go, Tom. Get what you can out of her. And we need to find out who the hell this fictional Zane is. Oh God, maybe he is the one that's her child and no one had any idea. Fucking hell. Dismissed."

Crane rose, thankful the meeting was over. As he reached the door Draper shouted at Crane's retreating back, "And don't come back unless you've some hard facts that will lead somewhere."

Thirty Five

By the time Crane arrived at Aldershot Police Station, Anderson had already phoned the Met and got permission to interview Janey Cunningham's mother.

"Their thinking is that it will save them a job and a trip out of London," said Anderson as he climbed into Crane's car.

"I wasn't waiting for permission, Derek," said Crane. "I'd have gone anyway."

"I know, but you're far more of a maverick than I am."

"No, I'm a detective in the British Army and determined to bring the killer of an army wife to justice."

"But it's the civilian police who will prosecute."

"I don't care who prosecutes, as long as someone does," Crane said.

"But there are rules, regulations and procedures to follow."

"I don't disagree, but that relates more to scenes of crime, forensics, chain of custody, as far as I can see. As long as I'm on active investigation I can interview who I like, when I like and where I like."

"I thought you'd say that," said Anderson.

"Anyway I'm under direct orders from my Captain to interview Mrs Carlton."

"I thought you'd say that too," he laughed.

Crane gunned the engine and roared away from the police station, not in the least bit bothered by Anderson's talk of policies and procedures. Realistically he knew he had to work with the police, but only up to a point and only with those policemen he wanted to work with. Saunders seemed alright, but no one from the Met had met Janey's mother and Crane hadn't any intention of letting them get within a mile of her, at least not until he'd talked to her.

Mrs Carlton opened the door and looked at them through red rimmed and bloodshot eyes. "Oh it's you two," she said and turned away from the open door.

They walked into the house after her and Crane closed the front door behind him. He found Anderson and Mrs Carlton sat in the same stuffy over-heated room as before, where she was surrounded by her photographs, which were all she had left of her daughter now. She was dressed in an old fashioned print dress, with an apron over the top of it and a cardigan on top of that, none of which matched either in colour or style. Crane wondered how she could wear so many clothes in the heat of the room. Perhaps you felt colder as you got older, he decided. As it was, he wished he could take his suit jacket off, as perspiration began to dribble down his neck.

"I had a visit from Reading Police yesterday," Mrs Carlton said. "To tell me my Janey was dead and that someone would be over today to talk to me about it. Is that you two?"

"Yes," said Anderson, "If you feel up to it."

"I thought you said you'd find her for me," she said. "That you didn't think anything bad had happened to her. Well you were bloody wrong there, weren't you?"

Crane couldn't actually remember promising her any such thing. And they had found her. It's just that she hadn't been alive when they had. But he kept his mouth firmly closed to stop any retort slipping through his lips. Now was not the time to alienate Mrs Carlton, they needed information from her.

"We are so sorry for your loss, Mrs Carlton," Anderson said. "Aren't we, Crane?"

"Absolutely," Crane joined in. "The thoughts of the British Army are with you at this difficult time. We'd be glad to send the Padre over, if you think it would help." Crane shut up at that point as Anderson kicked his ankle. Oh well, maybe that was going a bit too far, he conceded.

"Mrs Carlton, it seems that the autopsy turned up some information on your daughter that was unrelated to her death," Anderson said.

At the word 'autopsy' Mrs Carlton had begun to cry.

"I'm sorry if this is painful," he continued. "But we really do need to ask you some more questions about Janey. I'm sure you want to help us catch her killer, despite your distress."

Mrs Carlton pulled a tissue from under the sleeve of her cardigan, wiped her eyes and then blew her nose. Replacing it under her sleeve she said, "Of course. Sorry. What is it? What did they find?"

"Mrs Carlton, did you know that Janey had had a child?"

Anderson was rewarded with a watery smile. "Oh yes. Can you believe that had slipped my mind? It's just that it hasn't been spoken of since… well for nigh on

30 years now. I'd never thought about that. Maybe I'm not as alone as I'd imagined. Do you think you'll be able to find him for me?"

"Find who?" asked Crane, who couldn't keep quiet any longer, even at the expense of more bruises to his ankle.

"Why, Zane, my grandson."

Crane and Anderson stilled as the enormity of her casual words sunk in.

"Zane?" said Anderson in a strangled voice Crane had never heard before.

"Grandson?" Crane managed to croak.

"Oh my, it seems this calls for a cup of tea. It won't take a minute. I'd just boiled the kettle before you knocked," and it was a far happier woman who left them to their shock, than the one that had opened the door to them.

"What the hell?" hissed Crane when she'd left the room.

"I know," whispered Anderson. "But at least she seems willing to talk about it, him, Zane, or whatever his name is."

And then Crane collected another bruise to his ankle as Anderson kicked him to let him know Mrs Carlton was coming back.

Crane sprang up from the chair he was sitting in. "Here, let me help," he said and grabbed the tray from Mrs Carlton before she spilled even more tea. The tray was already swimming with murky brown liquid.

"Oh, thank you, my hands aren't as steady as they used to be."

Crane placed the tray on the table and he and Anderson ignored it. They didn't want tea. They wanted information from Mrs Carlton.

"So, Mrs Carlton," Anderson said. "You were going to tell us about your grandson?"

"It seems so long ago now," she said, her eyes misting over and her voice wobbling. "One day Janey came back from school. She was 15 if I remember correctly. Anyways, she was very upset and said that she was pregnant. She was starting to panic about it as someone had noticed at school. I asked her, what do you mean by noticed at school. In reply she lifted up her school jumper." Mrs Carlton closed her eyes, lost in the memory. "I couldn't believe it. She was clearly pregnant as she had a large bump. When I pressed her, she thought she was about five months gone. I nearly died I can tell you. She'd managed to hide it with large jumpers and shirts. She'd refused to do PE for ages. The school had sent home letters about it which she'd never given me and forged my signature on a note she wrote herself, requesting permission to be excluded from all games lessons, due to an undisclosed illness. I don't know," she said. "I used to hear of this sort of thing happening to other families, but I never thought it would happen to us."

Crane wondered how a mother could be so lax as to not notice that her daughter was pregnant, but once more kept that opinion to himself.

"So what happened then?" Anderson asked.

Crane was glad Anderson was doing the talking as he couldn't trust himself to be sympathetic.

"Well, of course, her father went ballistic, shouted and screamed at her, he did. Why didn't she tell us? Who was the father? That sort of thing. But Janey kept her mouth firmly closed. Anyway in the end we decided she should be kept home from school after that. We all thought it was for the best."

"For the best? For whom?" Anderson asked.

"Well Janey for one and for us as well, I suppose. Her reputation couldn't be tarnished with an unwanted baby. She was 15 at the time, for God's sake. What do you think we should have done?" Mrs Carlton snapped at Anderson.

"What happened to the baby?" Crane interjected to try and divert Mrs Carlton from her anger at Anderson.

"She went into a Catholic home for young mothers. After she'd given birth, they put the baby up for adoption and she came home. She said she'd called him Zane. And then none of us spoke of it again."

"Did she ever say anything about her son tracking her down?"

"Not to me, but then she was always so busy, we didn't get a chance to talk very often."

"Mrs Carlton, can you give us details of the facility Janey went to?"

"I think so, hang on," and she stood and walked over to a set of drawers. She rummaged around for a while then found a large brown envelope, which she carried back to her chair. "I'm sure it's in here," she said. Several pieces of paper later, she held up a letter. "Here, this is their confirmation that they had a place for Janey."

"May we keep this, please?" Anderson asked.

Mrs Carlton nodded. "But can I have it back?"

"Of course," Anderson soothed. "We'll be very careful with it."

They had just climbed into Crane's car when Anderson's phone rang. Anderson held up his hand to stop Crane driving away and listened for a moment.

"It's Saunders from the Met," he whispered to Crane who nodded and settled down in his seat to wait.

Anderson's end of the conversation didn't give much away, so Crane had to wait with mounting impatience while Anderson made notes in his book. He rapidly puffed on the cigarette he had lit, blowing the smoke out of his window.

At last Anderson ended the call and turned to Crane. "That was Saunders."

"And?" Crane's impatience was boiling over and he took one last drag of his cigarette.

"They've found the website Janey used for her escort services."

"And?" Crane threw the butt out of the window.

"They hope that he contacted her, or made a booking, through that agency."

"And? For God's sake, Derek!"

Anderson laughed at Crane's impatience, which made him even angrier.

"Sorry," Anderson apologised. "And they are going to follow up on that lead. They hope to be able to get a list of her clients from them and details of the credit cards that were used to make bookings with her."

"Can't we do that?"

"No. The Met are insisting that it falls within their remit and that they can get a search warrant quicker than we can if they need one. They reckon they'd be more intimidating to the owner of the website than us, or at least the local Aldershot police."

Crane blew out a sigh, "So what now?" Crane was deflating quicker than a pricked balloon.

"We follow our own lead. We need to investigate this Catholic home and see what we can find out about the adoption process, who Zane's adoptive parents were, etc."

"Right oh," Crane sighed. He knew better than to

challenge Britain's largest and best equipped police force. "So where to now?"

"Back to the police station. Let's see what we can find out about this home."

Thirty Six

It was early the next morning that DC Saunders rang, requesting a conference call with Crane and Anderson. Once the three of them were able to hear each other, Saunders brought them up to date.

"As you know," he began, "all crimes are put into the national database and from there we can search for those with similar modus operandi. Well, overnight I ran a search for murdered women with Janey Cunningham's description: blond hair, blue eyes, slim, long legged, murdered in and around the London area." Saunders paused.

"And you found one," stated Crane, his heart sinking. Why else would Saunders have phoned?

"Yes," Saunders confirmed. "Her body was found last month in the River Thames, just down from Taggs Island."

"Just one?" asked Anderson.

"Yes, but I've had a word with my boss and we're going to arrange for a search in the river around the island. With men on the banks and boats on the river at first and divers later if there is sufficient evidence that there may be more women down there."

"Sufficient evidence?" asked Crane.

"Normally we find shoes, or other items of clothing, stuck in reeds along the bank or under bridges that may be an indication of other victims."

The silence was heavy between the three men as they each thought about the possibility of finding more victims.

Crane broke it. "So you think that maybe our Zane has done this before?"

"It certainly fits the pathology of a psychopath. He could have started with women who looked like his mother."

"Practising," said Anderson.

"Precisely," agreed Saunders.

"Bloody hell," said Crane.

"And then once they failed to satisfy his need to kill his mother…"

"He found the opportunity to kill the real thing," said Crane.

"That's the working theory so far," agreed Saunders. "Look, I'll keep you up to date and I'm going to email to you the case notes and photographs. But I've got to ask you both to keep this under your hats for now."

"Of course," said Anderson.

"Absolutely," agreed Crane. "You'll let us know if you find any more bodies?"

"You'll be the first to know," said Saunders and cut the connection.

Crane slowly replaced the receiver and blew out a breath. Dear God, how much worse could this case get? If Saunders and his theories were correct, there could be several girls hidden in the Thames, lying in their silent, deep, watery graves, patiently waiting until they were found so that they could tell their secrets.

His computer dinged with the alert of an incoming email. Saunders had been quick about sending through the information and Crane reluctantly opened the attachment. Filling the screen was the image of a young girl, mid to late 20's, dead on the river bank. She was the spitting image of Janey Carlton at the same age. Only this girl had bits of leaves and plant lodged in her hair instead of artfully arranged blond locks. Her face was bloated, one eye nibbled out by some kind of fish or other. Her hands were placed by her side and Crane noticed there were only ribbons of flesh left on one or two of her fingers. Her legs looked bruised and putrefied. He closed his eyes against the photograph, wondering, not for the first time, why he did this job and went outside for a cigarette, before his morning briefing with Captain Draper.

As Crane paced around the car park outside Provost Barracks, he felt sick to his stomach and when he closed his eyes, a picture of his wife sprang to mind. However, it wasn't an image of Tina happy, healthy and smiling. But lying dead. A rotting corpse just like the picture he'd just looked at of the unknown victim, who might well have been killed by the elusive Zane. Opening his eyes again, he raised a shaking hand to his mouth to take a drag of his cigarette, but his fingers disobeyed his brain and the cigarette fell to the floor. Crushing it underfoot, he raised himself to his full height. He reminded himself that he was a soldier, who had a job to do and was under orders to do it to the best of his ability. He squared his shoulders against the vile images and rotated his head to try and release the tension in his neck. Being emotionally involved wouldn't do him, or the case, any good. Soldiers didn't do emotion. Emotion got you killed. It wasn't that he was a hard bastard; although that was the impression he gave. It was just that being a gibbering wreck, empathising with people's pain, feeling guilty about not saving someone when it clearly wasn't his fault, helped no one. He was a Sgt Major in the British Army. He had to show some backbone. Man up and help catch the bastard.

Thirty Seven

...*By now he had traced Janey and the Major to the Mayfair Club. It hadn't taken much effort. Once he was inveigled in their social set, albeit the fringes, all it took was a quiet word in a few ears, before someone told him about the Mayfair Club. Money being no object, he was welcomed by Dante Skinner with open arms and quickly became an enthusiastic member. He always went with a different girl on his arm and he quite literally, entered into the swing of things.*

For a few golden weeks he and whoever was his latest piece of totty became the preferred partners of choice for his mother and her husband, the Major. The Janey look-alikes attracted the Major and his dark, smouldering good looks, his mother.

He was in heaven. He relished her touch, revelled in it, and came alive in her arms. He worshiped her in the flesh whereas before he'd had to worship her from afar. He was careful to be the best sexual partner he could be. Putting her needs first, he teased, flirted and massaged her body and her ego. He told her how beautiful she was. How lucky the Major was to have her as his wife. Said he hoped her husband appreciated her as much as he did.

Janey responded as any woman would. She became as intoxicated with him as he was with her, although she always tried to hide that attraction from her husband. She said she didn't want him feeling jealous. But in the end he had been. Jealous, that was. He found ways to persuade his wife to find other partners. Janey told him the Major didn't wanted their experiences at the club to go stale. The idea was to sample new partners, not keep going to the same ones.

And so gradually Janey and the Major withdrew their favours from him. The army bastard took her away from him.

But he couldn't lose her. He had to find another way to get close to her again.

Thirty Eight

Crane was on the phone when Anderson arrived. They'd decided to meet at Provost Barracks, just for a change really and the policeman had arrived right on time.

As Crane put down the phone he said, "Great timing, Derek, that was Captain Draper on the phone. He'll be down shortly for an update."

Anderson nodded his assent and shrugged off his raincoat. Crane idly wondered whether he'd continue to wear it in the summer time. For some reason it was becoming a badge of honour for Anderson. Either that or he wore it because Crane himself wore a black raincoat, the dark colour making the army detective fade into the background and Anderson's beige fabric stand out.

Billy was just pouring coffee for them all, when Draper burst into the large room. He threaded his way through the desks and grabbed a coffee from the tray Billy was carrying. After blowing across the scalding liquid, he took a tentative sip and said, "Morning all, right where are we?"

The men gathered by Crane's whiteboards, which

Billy was religiously keeping up to date as information filtered in from the Aldershot and the Metropolitan Police forces.

"Let's start with the escort agency," said Anderson and rummaged in his briefcase. Pulling out several pages clipped together he said, "The Met have eventually got the information on the bookings for Janey Carlton."

"At last," said Crane.

Anderson ignored him. "They managed to trace the owner of the site she had a website hosted on."

"What does that mean?" asked Draper.

"When you build a website, you either use a large commercial site owner such Wordpress, or Webs; or someone designs one specifically for you. Janey chose a commercial site owner, one that specialised in her particular type of activities, where she built her site and it was hosted on their servers. They make it really easy to do by dragging and dropping text and picture boxes, contact forms and using their payment facilities."

"So," said Draper. "If someone goes on Janey's website and makes an appointment, they would use the payment facility on her website, which is controlled by the company that host it."

"That's right. So the Met managed to persuade the company to give them the list of payments made through her site."

"I guess her being found dead helped with that one," said Crane dryly.

Anderson threw him a look and continued, "Payments were made by credit card, to the Mayfair Club."

Crane abruptly sat down. "The lying bastard," he said.

"Who?" asked Draper also sitting.

"Dante bloody Skinner," said Crane.

"Exactly," agreed Anderson.

"He never said a word about running prostitutes on the side," said Crane. "But then he wouldn't do, would he?"

"No."

"Who?" asked Draper, so Crane explained that Dante Skinner was the owner of the Mayfair, where the Cunninghams and the other swingers gathered. Crane and Anderson had interviewed him. Twice.

"I don't know about you, Derek, but I'm fed up of people hiding things, keeping secrets. Dante Skinner could be harbouring a killer. Janey's mother didn't tell us about the baby. The Major didn't tell us about the drugs or sex. Jesus. What's wrong with these people?" he asked no one in particular.

"So despite the obstacles, which you've managed to hurdle, where do we go now?" Draper asked.

Anderson said, "The Met have sent through the list of clients identified from their credit card transactions. They got the information, as they have more clout than us, but it's down to us to help analyse it. I thought we could pull up a profile on each one of them and then it should be easy enough to find someone fitting our suspect criteria."

"Which is what?"

"Oh, right, boss, that's the other piece of news," said Crane. "Late yesterday we interviewed Mrs Carlton again and she told us that Janey had had a child when she was fifteen. He was put up for adoption and she'd asked the adoption agency that he be called Zane."

"Ah, I see," said Draper. "So we're looking for a male, aged around 30, going by the name of Zane."

"That's about right, boss. We've got an artist's impression of him from one of the couples who regularly attend the Mayfair."

"Get on with it then," Draper said, pushing himself out of his chair. He nodded to Derek as he walked away and disappeared back upstairs.

"That's it?" said Anderson. "That was the briefing?"

Crane nodded. "Why?" he asked.

"There was no investigative insight from him," said Anderson. "No try this, or try that, or what about this avenue of investigation. Just a 'get on with it'."

Crane smiled. "That's officers for you, Derek. Get used to it. I've had to."

Thirty Nine

Nothing much could be heard from Derek, Crane and Billy, apart from mumbles.

"How about him?" asked Anderson.

"Too old," commented Crane.

"Oh, right."

"Boss, this one?" said Billy.

Crane shook his head, "Wrong hair colour."

"Bugger."

Crane said, "Got a possible, here, Derek."

Anderson glanced over. "Too fat."

"Point taken," said Crane, who scratched at the scar under his beard. "I've never known a prostitute to have so many clients."

"Know a lot of them do you?" asked Anderson.

"You know what I mean, Derek, stop taking the piss."

"What I find surprising is how many of them use the wife's credit card, or at least a card in her name," said Anderson.

"Bet half the time she doesn't even know she has it!" said Crane.

"Too true." Anderson stood and stretched his spine.

"I don't know about you, but I need a sugar injection," he said.

"Wait a minute," called Crane. "I think I may have something here. Can you pull up this name on your terminal, Derek? You're remotely connected to the police databases aren't you?"

"Yup, pass it over. But only if Billy finds me something sugary to eat."

"Sorry?" said Billy who was also pouring over lists of credit card transactions, helping them out as he had a bit of free time and so had been pressganged into helping. "I never knew you could charge this much for sex," he said as he stood.

"Would you?" Crane asked him.

"What?"

"Pay for sex?"

Billy smiled, his blue eyes crinkling and his blond hair flopping forward. "Really? Seriously?"

"No, I don't suppose you'd ever need to," conceded Crane, whose dark features were the antipathy of Billy's blond hair, fresh-faced visage and crinkly blue eyes. With an impressive body, all rippling muscles and flat stomach, Billy was most women's dreamboat.

"That's about right, boss," he grinned. "So, cake or biscuits?"

"Both," said Crane and Anderson simultaneously.

"Well I'll be buggered," said Anderson as Billy walked away.

Crane wasn't sure how to take that comment; was it good news, or bad? So he asked.

"I think its good news," said Anderson. "Look at this, Crane."

Crane moved to view the terminal over Anderson's shoulder. "Who's that?" he asked as a picture of a

DVLC driving licence appeared on the screen. "My God, that looks like the artists' impression we have. Is it really Zane do you think?"

"Could well be, we'll have to check with them. Go and see them and show them a photograph."

"What's his name?" asked Crane.

"Tyler Wells, a resident in a trendy part of North London, employed as a Hedge Fund Manager in the City of London.

"Looks like we're off for another foray in the big smoke," said Crane gathering his things. "Don't forget your raincoat, Derek," and the two men got ready to leave as Billy stood watching them, holding three cups of tea and three slices of cake on a tray.

"Why, boss?"

"Why what?"

"Why are you off to London?"

"Are you going mad, Billy? We need to show Cynthia and Justin Hall the photo of Tyler Wells."

"Email it," said Billy, "that way you can have your tea and cake."

Crane and Anderson looked at each other and, having been exposed as technological dinosaurs, slunk back to their desks.

Forty

The view from the bank of the River Thames between East Molesey and Richmond was as beautiful as any landscape painting DC Saunders had ever seen. Lined with trees and pockets of grassy knolls it was a veritable piece of heaven. The sound of birdsong filtered through the trees, boats ran lazily up and down the river and from his position he had a view of Taggs Island, one of the most exclusive houseboat sites anywhere in the world, not just in England.

As he gazed at the structures, mostly two and three stories high, with banks of glass glinting in the sunlight, brightly coloured awnings and canopies hinting at gaiety and laughter, he tried to imagine what life would be like as a permanent resident on the river. Would you get seasick from the constant motion of the boats? Would you get annoyed at noise from neighbouring and passing boats? Or would it be a tranquil lifestyle, ideal for photographers and writers, artists and artisans? Either way it was probably better than life viewed from his own tiny bedsit in a converted warehouse in East London. In fact, truth be told, he didn't have a view at all, cheap rent being the trade-off for a window.

His roving eyes rested on the police launch moored just off the bank, from the Marine Policing Unit. This part of the river just fell into their remit, for which Saunders was grateful, as it made the job much easier, rather than contacting Surrey Police who used a launch provided by the Environment Agency. There was a man in the boat, the spotter for two divers who were exploring the river floor and river bank just beneath his feet, their buoys bobbing in the waves created by passing vessels on the other side of the river. They had been exploring the area for a couple of days now, but so far no other bodies had emerged. This was the last day of exploration, the Chief Investigating Officer having said that he was stretching the budget as it was and no way could they afford another day. If they drew a blank today, then that was it, the river would keep its secrets.

The emergence of a diver startled Saunders out of his musings, the black rubber suited man popping up out of the water like a jack in a box. His arm raised, he circled it, indicating he'd found something. Saunders had to contain his excitement, or was it dread, as the launch communicated with the two divers and the boat was brought into position. The divers submerged once more, the two of them working together to bring up whatever it was they'd found. Saunders leaned forward over the edge of the bank, desperately trying to see what was going on, but all that was in view was a few air bubbles reaching the surface from the divers below. After what seemed like eons, the water gushed and rushed before finally parting, revealing the divers and their catch. One seemed to be carrying a body and the other a chain tied to some sort of weight. As their grizzly cargo was transferred into the boat the radio

Saunders was carrying crackled into life.

"Body retrieved from the river bed, close to the bank, over."

"Can you tell if its male or female, over?"

"Female," came the distorted reply, "With long blond hair."

Saunders had been right. There was another one. He looked at his radio and opened his mouth to speak when the policeman on the launch began talking again.

"The lads say there's at least another one down there. Maybe two. The water's a bit murky at the moment from all the activity, so we're going to let it calm down and then try again in about an hour. Coming to shore with the body. Over and out."

Saunders stared at the launch as it made its way over to his position, not sure how he felt about being right. There were more bodies, more dead girls. But it didn't give him any pleasure, just hardened his resolve that they had to do everything in their power to catch the sick killer.

But his hardened resolve was no help when he saw the body the divers had brought up from her watery grave. As Saunders gazed at the girl laid out on a piece of black plastic, a rictus grin displaying her teeth and jaw bone as she had no lips left, her hair tangled and matted and torn out in places, he ran for the bushes. After he'd thrown up the numerous cups of coffee he'd consumed that morning, the bitter taste of bile lingered and he dug in his pockets for a packet of chewing gum. Somehow he managed to get the image of the dead body, of the as yet unknown girl, out of his thoughts. But one thing stayed with him. The rusty chain wrapped around her waist, attached to a square cube of concrete.

Forty One

Tyler Wells was in the middle of his morning. All around him colleagues beavered away. Phones rang, fists pumped and hands held heads in despair; all dependent upon the success or otherwise of their stock market portfolios. Their bodies were fuelled by adrenaline and the air charged with testosterone. Tyler was deep in thought. A new client had given him his portfolio to manage. A client who had a lot of money to invest, but expected quick results. It would require a steady nerve, sound judgment and more than a little bit of luck, but Tyler thought he might just be able to pull it off. He was looking at a list of companies that he'd highlighted as being 'ones to watch' and wondered if one or two of them would be a good fit for his new client.

"Mr Wells," said a voice behind him.

Tyler was aware of someone standing behind him and lifted his arm, a request that the man stop speaking. The last thing Tyler wanted at the moment was inane questions, or pleas for help from his colleagues. He continued to analyse the figures before him, ignoring the person standing behind him. A hand landing on his shoulder made him jump.

Turning around and shrugging the hand off, he said, "What the hell?"

"Tyler Wells?" the man asked.

Tyler had never seen the person who was speaking to him before and he looked at the man, taking in the squat muscly body, dark curly hair and close cropped beard. The man's blue eyes bored into him, the intense interest in them as piercing as a drill entering his brain, making Tyler flinch and look away.

"Yes, I'm Tyler Wells," he said and looked at the second man, registering the rumpled raincoat, messy grey hair and the badge of some sort that he was holding up. "Who the hell are you two?"

Tyler was still very much in work mode and extremely pissed off at being interrupted. He stood, not wanting the disadvantage of being lower than the two interlopers and having to look up at them.

"Sgt Major Crane, Royal Military Police," said the first.

"Detective Inspector Anderson," said the second, "Aldershot Police."

"What? Look, I don't know what you're doing here, but I have nothing at all to do with the military," he pointed at the man calling himself Crane, "and even less to do with Aldershot," he said to Anderson. "So if you wouldn't mind, I've got a lot of work to do before a meeting with a new client in," he glanced at his watch, "two hours. An extremely important meeting and one I have to be fully prepared for."

Tyler twisted away from the two men, mumbled, "Idiots," under his breath and sitting down bent once more over the papers on his desk.

"I don't think you quite understand, sir," said one of

them, grabbing Tyler's arm and lifting him from his seat.

"Get your fucking hand off me," said Tyler, trying to shake off the meaty paw of the military man, who held on with the tenacity of a terrier and the grip of a python.

"Tyler Wells," said the policeman, "You are under arrest on suspicion of the murder of Janey Cunningham, nee Carlton. You are to accompany us to Aldershot Police Station."

Tyler watched the detective who was still talking, saying something about rights and defence, but it wasn't really going in. He looked around the room, to find he was the subject of everyone's interest. Ringing phones were going un-answered, people were standing up whispering amongst themselves and some of his colleagues who sat close to Tyler's desk, were physically distancing themselves from him, by retreating to the groups of people that had formed to watch the drama unfolding before them.

Tyler continued to struggle, trying to work his arm free from Crane's grip. He turned to face his captor and drew his arm back to punch the army detective in the face, when it was grabbed and twisted behind his back. Tyler could hear the jingle of the handcuffs as they were attached to first one wrist and then the other, immobilising his hands and arms. Their grip around his wrists felt as heavy as the chains the ghost of Marley wore in 'A Christmas Carol' and Tyler began to realise that something was terribly wrong, something that he wouldn't be able to get out of easily. He was trapped in a scenario worthy of any nightmare. Angry tears began to form, that Tyler couldn't swipe away, so he coughed, swallowed hard and looked at the rumpled detective.

"I can't believe you are doing this, embarrassing me in front of my work colleagues, accusing me of murder." Tyler turned as Crane pushed him out of the way and began to collect items from Tyler's desk.

"Look," he pleaded. "I haven't done anything wrong! Please, I need to tell my wife, let me call her, she'll tell you I haven't done anything."

When neither man spoke and began to drag him along the walkway of the large office, towards the exit, he tried again, fear making his voice rise an octave. "I want a solicitor. I'm allowed a phone call."

Tyler wasn't at all sure of that last one, but thought it sounded good. Also he didn't have a solicitor, at least not one that dealt with criminal cases, but they weren't to know that.

"Where are we going?" he asked as they pushed through the double doors out of the large open plan space and waited at the bank of lifts. He noticed that Crane was holding the items that had been collected from his desk; laptop, mobile phone, suit jacket, diary and his watch which he had taken off whilst working, as it irritatingly clanged against his keyboard.

"It will all become clear in due course," the policeman said, the ominous words weighing heavily on Tyler's mind, as he was escorted out of the building and into a waiting car.

All the way to Aldershot, along the M3 motorway and then local dual carriageways, Tyler racked his brains to think of anything at all that could get him out of the bloody mess he'd found himself in. Crane and Anderson had been silent all the way there, the atmosphere in the car full of their expectation and Tyler's fright. His arms pinned uncomfortably behind him, forced Tyler to sit crushed in the corner of the car, between the back seat and the door, the only way he could keep upright as they sped around corners and overtook traffic. He was sure his wrists and hands were marked with red sores, where the handcuffs bit deeply into his skin from the pressure of his body.

Upon their arrival at Aldershot Police Station, he was taken to an interview room and sat in a plastic chair. Anderson removed the handcuffs and then he was left alone with his thoughts. Tyler immediately began inspecting his wrists, rubbing at the deep red marks and his red raw skin. As his body was stiff from the car journey, he walked around the room, shaking his legs and arms to get his circulation going. Blood flow was good. Blood to his head was good. It would help him think. Help him find a way out of this mess.

Forty Two

…So that was the end of that. The Major and Janey no longer wanted him and his latest glamour girl as their partners of preference and he was left with the dregs of the clientele, not one of whom could hold a candle to his Janey.

Fed up with the situation, he knew he had to find another way. The computer system of the Mayfair Club was easy enough to crack for someone with his hacking abilities. It took him precisely 15 minutes. He'd timed himself. Once there he began to rummage around, clicking on various files and infiltrating deep into their records.

He found video clips and photographs, secretly taken of the unsuspecting members, something Dante Skinner no doubt kept as insurance or for darker purposes. He wondered how many of his perverted clients would pay good money to have their activities cleansed from the Mayfair Club hard drives.

Having amused himself with the images, he grew bored and flitted around the system, until he found a section devoted to 'Park Lane Escorts'. Leaving the computer for a moment, he crossed the living room, poured himself a glass of scotch and then settled down once more at his computer. The Park Lane Escorts website proved to be the mother lode he'd been looking for.

He recalled once having asked Janey how she managed to find the time for their extracurricular activities at the club, what with her busy work schedule and all. She'd laughed. But it came out sounding bitter and harsh; a laugh that held no mirth, only the acrimonious sound of failure. She'd said that over the past couple of years the work had dried up. It seemed she was in that dark chasm between youth and maturity. Too old for most of the cosmetic and clothing companies, yet not old enough to be the mature woman. It seemed this sorry state of affairs could go on for a few years yet and so she'd had to turn to other avenues of revenue. When pressed and asked what they were, she wouldn't say. But now it seemed he'd found out her secret.

There she was. His Janey. Loving the camera as she did, her pictures were meant to draw in and entice a prospective client and they did that in spades. She was practically making love to the damn lense. All sexy underwear, tousled hair, sucked in cheekbones and pouting lips, who could resist such a woman? Certainly not him. She was definitely high class, no doubt about it, with a high class price to match. But no matter, for after all, this time it wouldn't be his own money that he was spending. It was time to book an appointment with her.

He opened the drawer in his desk and withdrew the credit card details belonging to his brother, who had unsuspectingly opened a keyboard logger virus which had been buried in an attachment to an email. This had kindly given up his credit card details after an on-line purchase had been made. The security code on the back of the card had been what he had specifically been after. Turning back to his keyboard he was disappointed to find there wasn't an open slot with Janey until the following week. But it was of no matter. The anticipation would bolster him. By the time they did meet, he would be bursting with anticipated lust. Just the way she liked him.

Forty Three

Wanting to make sure they had their game plan synchronised, Crane and Anderson let Tyler endure an interminable wait while they prepared. From the look of him, he wasn't handling it well, thought Crane as he watched Tyler through the viewing screen. Tyler examined his surroundings (bare and uninviting, with three chairs and one table the only furniture); tried the door (locked); shook his limbs out (as though he had a bad case of pins and needles); firstly ran his fingers through his hair and then drummed then on the table.

Anderson arrived at Crane's side and said, "How's he doing?"

"I think we've timed it perfectly. He is anxious, distracted, worried and keeps shouting for his wife and his solicitor."

"Let's do it then," and Anderson picked up the file he had compiled on Tyler Wells and the two men went into the interview room.

"Thank God!" Tyler stood at their arrival. "Perhaps now you can explain to me what the hell is going on."

"Of course, sir," said Anderson, as though surprised by Tyler's comment. "That's precisely why we're here."

"Oh. Right," said Tyler and Crane smiled to himself as Anderson had immediately wrong-footed the suspect.

"Please sit down."

"What? Oh, yes."

As Tyler complied, Anderson opened the file in front of him, took out a piece of paper and passed it to Tyler.

"Could you please confirm that this is a copy of your credit card statement?"

"What?" Tyler grabbed the paper and scanned it. "How did you get this? You can't get stuff like this without a warrant surely!"

"You're absolutely right," said Crane. "We can't. That's why we got one."

"Got one! What? How? Why?"

"The Metropolitan Police organised it for us," explained Crane. "They got a warrant, searched your property, interviewed your wife and emailed several pieces of paper over for us that they thought could be useful to the investigation."

"They also took items from your house that could be of interest for testing," added Anderson with a smile.

"Testing? What the hell for?"

"Let's just say forensic testing at the moment, shall we," and Anderson looked at Crane who nodded his agreement. "So, back to the matter in hand. Your credit card statement. You can confirm it's yours?"

"What?" Tyler was still blustering. Crane nodded to himself approvingly. They definitely had him on the back foot.

"Please, sir, let's not make this interview any longer than it has to be," said Anderson, still being unfailingly polite. "You wanted to know what this was all about.

Well, it's about those three transactions highlighted on that statement. They are payments to the Mayfair Club for £1,000 each."

Tyler peered at the paper as though he'd never seen it before, but in the end he had to nod his agreement.

Crane said, "This statement has been confirmed as relating to this physical credit card."

Anderson obliged by taking that out of the file also. "Which was taken from your wallet when we arrested you."

"So?" said Tyler.

Crane wasn't sure if the question was borne out of bluster, or fright, but the transactions clearly meant something to Tyler as he had stopped making eye contact with them and instead intensely studied the table.

"The transactions were for several appointments to see Janey Cunningham, nee Carlton and were payments for sex. The last appointment was immediately before her approximate time of death. The payments were made through her website which is controlled by the Mayfair Club, hence that name appearing on your credit card statement."

Tyler Wells had gone from being red faced with anger, to white with shock when told that they had searched his house, to his current grey visage, which reminded Crane of wet cement.

"You're talking about that woman who went missing, aren't you?" Tyler asked. "The model. That's why you're here," he pointed at Crane. "Her husband is in the army. Major someone or other. I saw it on the news."

"Cunningham," confirmed Crane. "Major Cunningham." Crane leaned across the desk, being deliberately threatening. "You seem to know quite a bit about the case, Mr Wells. Following it are you? Watching the news every evening, trying to catch even the smallest of items about her? I bet you read every paper you can get your hands on, as well. I've met killers like you before. They need verification of their abilities. Need to bask in the glory of the publicity they are generating."

Tyler sat back in his chair, open mouthed, but silent. Trembling in fear like a mouse cornered by a cat.

"Was seeing her at the Mayfair Club not enough for you?" Anderson asked.

"Eh?"

"You've been identified by people who regularly attend the Mayfair Club, as a customer named Zane. It's a swingers club, where in the past you were a regular sexual partner of Janey Cunningham."

"Zane? Who the hell is Zane?"

"Weren't you listening, Mr Wells? Zane is the name you used at the Mayfair Club."

Crane did his leaning-in thing again saying, "I take it you couldn't get enough of her? What was it? Was she bored with you? Wouldn't sleep with you anymore so you had to pay for it? Three times? Her husband has confirmed that you came on too strong at the club, that he thought you were creepy, obsessed. Oh and by the way," continued Crane settling back in his chair and dropping another bomb, "He's identified you as the man he and his wife knew as Zane as well."

"Stop! Stop it!" Tyler shouted standing and holding his hands over his ears. "Her husband? I've never met him. I've never met any of them."

"Sit down!" It was Anderson's turn to shout.

"Now!" bellowed Crane.

Wells looked from one to the other, to the door, to the glass viewing panel, as if desperate to flee, but of course there was nowhere for him to go. So he sat down, as instructed, slouching in his chair, emotionally spent, wiping tears from his face in a scrubbing motion.

"Where were you on the night of her murder?" Anderson asked.

Crane was glad they were getting to this part of the interview. To be honest he was a bit wrung out himself. He couldn't decide whether Tyler Wells really didn't know what they were talking about, or was a bloody good actor. His fear could be from getting caught, just as easily as from being wrongly accused.

"When?"

Anderson supplied the date.

Tyler heaved a resigned sigh. "I don't bloody know. At home I expect, with my family, where I normally am when I'm not at work."

"Well your wife remembers. Or at least she knows where she was. She was away with the children visiting her parents. You were at home, alone."

That wound Tyler up, as though Tyler had a key in his back and Anderson had obligingly turned it.

"You've talked to my wife? How dare you! Leave her out of this!"

"Out of what?" cut in Crane. "Your obsession with Janey Carlton? Your murder of Janey Carlton?"

"I haven't murdered anyone, I've never met her, and I don't know what you're talking about."

Tyler had begun to cry again, but this time the tears ran down his face unchecked and trickled along his neck to soak into his shirt collar.

Anderson said, "That isn't a very novel approach, Mr Wells. I would have thought someone of your intelligence would have come up with a better excuse than that. Simple minded criminals say they are innocent all of the time and guess what?"

"What?"

"We don't believe them either."

The two detectives said nothing and Crane watched as the vocalisation of their disbelief shut out the small ray of hope Tyler Wells had left; hope that this was all some dreadful mistake. He closed his eyes and shook his head.

Then, coughing to clear his throat, he said, "Right that's it. I've had enough. I want my solicitor. I'm not saying another word until I get one."

Anderson closed his file and said, "Very well. Your wife's organising that. I expect someone will be here soon or maybe not so soon. You know what the traffic is like at this time of day."

"I'd also like to go to the bathroom and I want something to drink."

"Of course. How about a good book as well to help pass the time?" Crane said sarcastically as he stood, "A good murder mystery perhaps?"

Forty Four

Ken Brown, the Marine Police Unit officer thought that it was highly likely that the bodies had been dropped into the river from another site and made their way towards the bank where they were found.

"What do you mean?" DC Saunders asked. "The girls were weighted down. Wouldn't they have just sunk and stayed there?"

"Not necessarily," came the reply. "With the tide, currents, passing vessels and such, it is highly likely that they were swept up in the wake, the weights bumping along the bottom and coming to rest here."

Saunders deliberately avoided looking at the three girls who had been rescued from the Thames. Well, not rescued exactly, but liberated at least. They were in various stages of decomposition, even Saunders could see that, and the pathologist had promised he would try and identify which girl had gone in first and give them a possible time line. But it would take some work back at the mortuary, so not to expect results straight away.

"Any ideas where they came from then?" Saunders gazed out over the now peaceful waters.

"I reckon there is as good a place as any," Brown

said, pointing to the island just upstream from them. "I reckon you should start with Taggs Island."

"How in hell am I supposed to get there?" Saunders looked with dismay at the bridge leading to the island, which was on the opposite bank of the Thames. Having to drive round would take him ages.

"I'll give you a lift," the man grinned and walked towards the police launch. "Hop in."

Saunders sat behind the officer, who was dressed in what could best be described as army fatigues in blue and whose bald head seemed to gleam in the weak sunshine that was breaking through the grey clouds. Brown had given him a glimmer of hope. If the girls had come from Taggs Island, at least it was a line of enquiry. Someone may have seen something, heard something, or noticed the strange behaviour of a neighbour. Anything at all would be good, for they had bugger all else.

As they pulled up into a small break between the houseboats, Saunders clambered out and waved his thanks to Brown. Scrabbling up the bank he came face to face with a woman who was watching him, consternation written all over her face, clearly wondering what the hell he was doing.

"Afternoon," he called as he pulled himself upright, after slipping on yet another wet patch of mud. "Wonder if you can help me?" he asked, grabbing his identification out of his pocket. "DC Saunders, Metropolitan Police, is there, um, anyone in charge here?"

"In charge?" the woman looked askance. "Well, I suppose you could talk to a committee member," she said, stuffing her hands in the pocket of her fleecy jacket. "What's it about?"

"I'd rather not say at the moment. Can you point me in the direct of a committee member then?"

"I think Jeff is in," she said. "He's in The Falcon, three boats down," and she turned and pointed downstream. "The only way to get there is to walk through this gap here to where the gardens end. Turn to your left and walk along the track. There's a sign up with the name of his boat on it, so you can't miss it. Walk through his garden to the front door."

'Front door' seemed an incongruous phrase in relation to a boat, but Saunders did as she asked. As he walked, he looked around in amazement at the gardens accompanying the houseboats. Some were large with garages and sheds, others small with tiny lawns and flowers. Some boats were hidden behind trees and hedges, others exposed to the track. He wasn't sure what he'd expected, but was pretty sure it wasn't something as suburban as this. If anything, he'd just expected a kind of tow path and the boats plonked alongside it, rather like a canal bank. Turning into the garden marked with the name 'The Falcon', Saunders walked into one of the smaller gardens and up to the front door. From this side, the houseboat looked just like a house. A two story dwelling with a pitched roof. You couldn't see the river. The only indication it was on the river being mooring lines stretching from each end of the structure, tying the boat securely to the bank.

His knock was answered by a man Saunders thought was probably mid 50's, with a wiry body; but could have been older, as his weather beaten face indicated. He had on a blue smock affair of the type sailors wore, over jeans and navy deck shoes.

"Yes?" the man said.

Saunders introduced himself and said he was looking

for a committee member named Jeff. Once the man had confirmed that was him, he was invited on board. If Jeff Buckley said anything else, Saunders didn't hear it. They walked into a living room that stretched the full width of the boat and the wall facing the river was made up of glass panels. Saunders stared in amazement as the weak sunshine streamed in, the glass magnifying the light, so the sunbeams filled the large room, glinting off round, metal-edged port holes and sunken lights in the ceiling. The furniture was large and comfortable and Buckley indicated an easy chair, which Saunders sank into.

"I'm afraid we've had a find of sorts on the opposite bank, just downstream from here," Saunders said, pulling himself together and drawing his eyes away from the windows.

"Mmm," Jeff murmured, "I noticed the activity. Been at it most of the day haven't you?"

"Yes, not the best job I've ever been on."

"So what did you find?" Jeff played with his long dark hair, which hung to his shoulders and was highlighted with grey streaks.

"I'm not at liberty to say at the moment, sir, but suffice it to say we'll need to be interviewing the residents, tomorrow most likely."

"Sounds like you've found a body to me," Jeff said looking at Saunders closely.

But Saunders didn't reply to that comment, saying instead, "How many boats are there moored around the island?"

"62. We're all registered with TIRA, the Taggs Island Residents Association and the association owns, and is responsible for, the island. I'm one of the committee members."

"I'll need a list of all the residents, please."

Jeff seemed to ponder this request, taking his time before answering. "We're very private people here," he said. "I'm not sure I should be giving you that sort of information."

"That's as maybe, but I'm going to have to insist."

"It's serious then, your 'find'," and Jeff motioned towards the river with his head.

"Very."

"Alright, give me a minute," and Buckley stood and left the living room and could be heard walking through the boat.

Saunders stood and admired the view for a while. He heard mumblings from the other end of the houseboat and assumed Buckley was checking his request with another committee member. But it wasn't long before the man returned with pieces of paper in his hand.

"Can I ask that you keep this information confidential and that you can confirm it is only used as part of your enquiry?" he asked.

"Absolutely, sir," said Saunders and took the proffered papers. "How many of the residents own a small boat?"

"Most of us have small rowing boats or ones with an outboard motor, that's nothing unusual here. We are a water based community. The only way in is via a boat, or the small bridge linking the island to the mainland. Look that's what I mean."

Saunders watched a resident puttering over from the opposite bank of the River Thames. As the small vessel drew near, Saunders could see shopping bags on the floor of the boat. The man arrived at his home, tied up the boat, got out and pulled out three bulging carrier bags from a well-known supermarket. Who'd have thought such a life possible, only a few miles from the centre of London, Saunders thought to himself.

"That reminds me, how am I going to get back over there? I came on the police launch," he said.

With a chuckle Jeff said, "No worries, I'll take you back," and pointed to a small rowing boat moored alongside.

Forty Five

After a well-earned fag break, Crane walked back through Aldershot Police Station to Anderson's office and found the policeman sitting at his desk with a bunch of papers in his hand.

"Oh, there you are," said Anderson. "These have just come through from the Met."

"What are they?"

"Papers and correspondence found in Wells' house."

Sitting down, Crane asked, "Anything of interest?"

"Well, the usual mortgage documents, insurance policies and birth certificates for his kids."

"Any birth certificate for him?"

"Hang on," and Anderson flicked through the pile.

"Here we are," he said. "But it's not a birth certificate," and he handed it to Crane.

"What is it then?"

"It's a certified copy of an entry in the Adopted Children Register, which is the equivalent of a birth certificate for an adopted child."

Crane smiled, slowly. "Adopted, eh?"

Anderson nodded and shouted for a passing detective constable, "Oh, Simon,"

"Yes, Guv?" asked the young man, who Crane was sure should still be a school.

"Trace this set of parents for me would you?" said Anderson and Crane handed the lad the copy of the Adoption Certificate.

"But… I was just going for lunch."

"And now you're not. Right?"

A flush crept up the young man's face. "Right, Guv."

"Excellent, you've got five minutes," he called to the DC's retreating back. Turning once more to Crane, he said, "We've not had any word through from the Catholic home that arranged for the adoption of Janey's child, they are still stalling. So are the adoption authorities. So maybe we can get some information from Wells' adoptive parents. Perhaps they know who Tyler's birth mother is."

"Isn't there some way of adoptive children being able to trace their birth parents?"

Anderson nodded his agreement. "Yes, several ways, but they are all insistent that the only people they assist are the birth parents and the child of those parents. They won't help anyone else, not even the police. Adoption records are very closely guarded; otherwise people won't have faith in the system. It ensures anonymity for the parent whilst the child is growing up. Once a child reaches 18 he or she can start looking for their birth parents, but that parent always has the option of not wanting to be identified or the choice to accept or reject a child who reaches out to them. And visa versa, of course."

"I wonder if Janey ever reached out to her child."

"I shouldn't think so, not someone in her position, well known, rich, successful and very visible in the media. The fall-out would probably affect her career and as it was doing badly already…" Anderson let the words hang.

Exhaling a deep breath, Crane said, "Yes, I guess you're right. But that may be one of the reasons she became so flaky. You know, drugs, alcohol, sex. Maybe her adopted child played on her mind as well as the downward spiral of her career."

"It seems to me she was on a pretty downward spiral herself, becoming more and more extreme in her search for gratification."

"Pretty fucked up, really," said Crane and finished the last of his coffee, just as the young DC came back.

"Here you are, Guv, details on Mr and Mrs Wells. Both alive, both retired, no criminal records, residing in Surrey."

"Thanks," said Anderson taking the proffered piece of paper. At the young man's raised eyebrow he said, "Off you go to lunch, then," and was rewarded with a grateful smile.

"So Tyler seems to have been adopted by a middle class couple and had a good upbringing."

Anderson nodded. "That's what I suspected. The thing that bothers me is that he doesn't seem the type."

"The type?"

"The type to go around finding his birth mother, sleeping with her and then killing her."

"Why, just because he's got a lot of money and went to a good school?"

"No, it's not just that. He does seem to be what he claims to be; a family man who works hard to support them and to give his children a good start in life."

"So you think his fear of us is because he didn't kill Janey Cunningham and is being wrongly accused as he keeps saying. Not because he's afraid he's been caught."

"Yes, something like that."

"Well, there's one way we'll know for sure," said Crane.

"DNA," said Anderson.

"Exactly. And if he's as innocent as he claims, then he shouldn't have a problem giving us a sample of his DNA, to give us solid proof that it wasn't his semen inside Janey."

"Let's go and see what he says then, shall we?" said Anderson getting up.

Forty Six

Tyler had never been so happy to see a solicitor. Not that he'd had many dealings with one in the past, only using a local firm when he and Penny had moved house, or when they'd made their wills. He didn't know the man, but that didn't dampen his enthusiasm. Just the contact from another human being who was on his side and would help him get out of this Godforsaken place and home to his wife and kids, was enough.

Penny had been on his mind a lot. How was she taking this? Did she believe in his innocence? Would she be at home waiting for him when he got out? All he could see when he closed his eyes were her fine features, flowing blond hair and supple body. So great was his need to see her again that his whole body ached. He supposed that if nothing else, on his part at least, the separation and frightful situation that he'd found himself in had made him realise just how much he loved her. He had been far more shaken by the experience of being arrested than he'd first admitted to himself. He'd thought he could brazen it out, imagined he could be the same confident person as he was at work, in control, admired, respected. But all those attributes of his seemed to have vanished like morning mist burned off by the sun that was the scrutiny of the police.

To start with, the solicitor had asked him more or less the same questions as the police had, but this time it was different, for the man was on his side, not theirs. Tyler had had to admit to not having an alibi on the night in question, but with probing enquiries from his solicitor, was able to remember additional details, such as what time he'd left work, what train he'd caught and that one of the neighbours had seen him as he walked home. The solicitor wanted to know if he had he made any phone calls that night? If so to whom and at what time?

Looking at Charles Walker, the young, dapper man sitting opposite him, who was from one of London's finest law firms and had been retained by Tyler's employers, he said, "I'm adopted."

"I know," said Charles.

"You do?" Tyler was startled by the admission. "Who told you?"

It wasn't something that Tyler was ashamed of, he just never talked about it, much preferring to keep the illusion that his mother and father were his birth parents. There was no need for anyone to know outside the immediate family. It was Tyler's way of blocking out his past, blocking out the mother who had abandoned him. He loved his adopted parents fiercely, feeling that the more he loved them, the less likely they were to leave him.

"The police," Charles replied. "They found your adoption certificate at your home."

"What does that have to do with anything?"

"I see you gave a DNA sample," Charles deflected

Tyler's question.

"Yes, I've nothing to hide," Tyler sat up straighter in his chair, convinced that his innocence would be confirmed by the DNA test.

"Well, my advice would have been not to."

"Why ever not?"

"It would have slowed them down. The need for them to get a warrant to take it, would have taken some time and given us some breathing space. But they'd have got it in the end."

"I thought it would prove my innocence," stressed Tyler. "Show it wasn't me."

"Ah." Charles Walker sat back in his chair and put his pen on his notebook.

The action frightened Tyler.

"It's not as simple as that I'm afraid."

Confirming his fear.

Tyler closed his eyes. If ever there was a 'beam me up Scotty' moment it seemed this could be it. "Why?" he whispered.

"The police have disclosed to me that the DNA found on Janey Cunningham's body was a familial match."

Tyler's eyes snapped open. "What?"

Charles nodded. "They think the killer was her son and as you're adopted…. Well I don't have to paint a picture for you."

It couldn't be, surely not. "But I don't even know who my mother is! Are they saying Janey Cunningham was my mother? This is unthinkable, unbearable!"

Tyler sprung to his feet and began walking around the room, a cornered animal, pacing backwards and forwards as he realised he had nowhere to go. Realised he was trapped.

"Please, Tyler, sit down. Let's continue. I've still got more questions."

Tyler slowly nodded and moved back to his chair, slumping onto it, spent, defeated.

"What about the credit card transactions?" Charles asked.

"I hadn't used the credit card to pay for a hooker. I found the payments on my statement and reported them to the card company. You can ask them. Check with them. My phone call will be on their records."

"Did they agree with you that someone had stolen your card details?" Charles asked, scribbling away.

"Well, no, actually, they didn't."

"Why?" Charles stopped writing and looked up.

"They said it was used over the phone, or via the internet, with the physical card not seen, but the correct security code had been given, so they passed the transaction. Three times." Tyler caught the shadow of doubt in Charles' eyes and quickly said, "But there is something that I think could help."

Tyler told him about seeing a man who looked just like him and the fact that someone had been in his house. Twice.

"Well, that all very interesting, but without any corroboration it won't help. You could just be claiming someone had been in your house. Did you tell Penny?"

"No, I didn't want to frighten her. But what about the man I saw?"

"Tyler, you could just have seen your own reflection in the shop window."

The faint tendrils of hope that had been blossoming shrivelled and died. No one believed him. Not even his solicitor.

"What happens now?" he asked.

"The police haven't got much physical evidence and the results of the DNA testing won't be in for a while, so I should be able to get bail for you. But they'll take your passport and you'll have to report in fairly regularly to your local police station. But at least you'll be able to go home while we work all this out."

Tyler nodded. "You will be able to? Work it out?" one last ditch attempt to fan the flames of hope.

But the solicitor didn't say anything. His silence was more eloquent than any words. In his head Tyler heard the clang of the prison gates closing behind him and sealing his fate.

Forty Seven

"Alright, Derek, I'm here. What's the emergency?"

Crane had been responding to a phone call from Anderson, requesting his attendance at Aldershot Police Station. 'Drop everything and come over', was the message Billy gave him, so Crane had complied.

"This better be good, I was in a briefing with Draper," he said as he walked through Anderson's office door.

"Oh, it is, Crane. It really is," and Anderson took a joyous bite of the biscuit he was waiving in the air.

"Don't tell me, you're giving up sugar? Or has Mrs Derek thrown away your raincoat again and you've found it?" Crane joked as he moved files from a chair to the floor, so he could sit down.

"Idiot," mumbled Anderson through biscuit crumbs. Swallowing and then slurping some tea, he said, "The DNA results from Tyler Wells are back."

Crane smiled. "Ah, so that's the reason for this celebration?"

Anderson nodded, "Most definitely."

A sense of achievement washed over Crane. At last the case was about to be closed. They were close to arresting Janey Cunningham's killer. The army would be pleased. Very pleased indeed and, to be fair, so would Major Cunningham. For even though the focus had recently been taken off him and suspicion fallen onto Tyler Wells, there had always been that seed of doubt in Crane's mind. Doubt as to Tyler's guilt. Doubt as to the Major's innocence. He was glad to be getting rid of this case. He was fed up of lifting up rocks and finding dark secrets and strange behaviours underneath each of them.

Anderson handed Crane the report. "There's a lot of scientific waffle, but the bottom line is that the DNA sample from Tyler Wells is a match to that of the semen taken from Janey Cunningham."

"And it's confirmed as a familial match?"

"No doubt at all," Anderson smiled. "Piece of cake?" He offered Crane the plate sat next to his cup of tea.

"Don't mind if I do, Derek," grinned Crane and for a moment the two men munched quietly on the celebratory treat.

Two quick phone calls later; the first one to Tyler's Wells' office confirming his presence at work and the second to DC Saunders at the Met, advising they were going to arrest Tyler Wells and the two men were ready to leave for the City. Crane remembered the last time they'd gone there to arrest Tyler. Then it was on suspicion of murder. This time it would be for murder. There was no way out for Tyler now. He was wriggling on Crane's hook and this time Crane had no intention of throwing his catch back into the river.

Walking out of the police station, their determination visible in every stride, they were stopped by someone calling their names.

"Mr Anderson! Mr Crane!"

They stopped. Both were surprised that someone would call to them and not use their ranks. Turning back towards the building, they saw Mrs Carlton hovering by the door.

"Oh, Mr Anderson, I'm so glad I caught you," she said.

"Detective Inspector," said Anderson.

"Quite. And Mr Crane."

"Sgt Major," corrected Crane.

"Sorry, I couldn't remember your titles, only your surnames."

"It's alright," conceded Crane. "How can we help?"

Crane remembered the poor broken woman she'd been the last time they had met and decided some compassion for the victim's mother wouldn't go amiss. And Tyler Wells wasn't going anywhere. They could take a few minutes to hear her out.

"The nice man inside said you'd just left. It took all of my courage to come here, I can tell you, and I just have to see you right now."

The three formed a small huddle in the car park.

Anderson said, "What is it, Mrs Carlton? We've just had a break in the case and I…" at Crane's kick he changed that to "…we will be coming to see you tomorrow to explain what is happening. So if you don't mind…" Derek pointed to his car.

"That's why I had to come and see you. It's about the case. I've some information for you. I think it could be quite important." Mrs Carlton dropped her eyes to the floor. "I know I should have told you before, but…" She stopped talking, her eyes becoming moist and she held her shopping bag up against her chest.

"Told us what?" Crane had a bad feeling about this.

Why was the woman so intent on talking to them? Was there yet another skeleton in the cupboard?

"It's alright, Mrs Carlton," said Anderson. "Is it about your daughter?"

Mrs Carlton nodded.

"Is it something that could help find her killer?"

Again the nod. Mrs Carlton wrapped her arms around her bag and cradled it as if it were a child. Or was it a defence mechanism? Crane couldn't decide.

Looking at a point somewhere over Anderson's shoulder Mrs Carlton said, "Janey had two babies."

Anderson's eyes bulged.

Crane managed to croak, "Two? She was pregnant twice?"

"No, Mr Crane, my Janey had twins. Identical twins."

Forty Eight

"I think we better go inside," said Anderson and taking Mrs Carlton by the elbow, he led her back into Aldershot Police Station. Five minutes earlier they had been full of excitement, about to arrest a murderer. Now they were now returning to the building, confused, exasperated and empty handed.

Once Mrs Carlton had been settled into an interview room and provided with a sweet cup of tea to calm her nerves, Crane gave vent to his frustration in the corridor outside.

"Jesus, Derek. What is it with these people? Their whole lives are built on lies, on shifting sands. I don't think I've ever met a family like it."

"I'm not sure I have either. I know a fair few criminal families that keep secrets and tell lies, but at least everyone knows they're bent. This lot, they're always pretending to be something, or someone, that they're not."

Crane tried to get everything straight in his head and said, "Janey Carlton had identical twins. They must have been separated at birth. Tyler was adopted by a nice middle class couple, Mr and Mrs Wells. The other, who could possibly really be called Zane, well we don't know what happened to him. We have to get some information out of that Catholic Home."

"We're not getting anywhere with them. They are flatly refusing to disclose any information whatsoever."

"I think they need telling that if they don't give us something, an innocent man could be convicted of murder."

"Do you think Tyler's innocent now?"

"To be honest, Derek, I've no bloody idea. But maybe this confession from his grandmother at least makes his arguments for his innocence plausible."

"How so?"

"Well, we now know there does seem to be someone called Zane and that someone looks identical to Tyler. It is also possible that this mysterious twin brother could have hacked into Tyler's accounts and stolen his identity. It makes Tyler's story about someone stalking him have a ring of truth in it."

"But what about the DNA?"

"Good point. We need to ask questions of the experts about that."

"What for? The DNA is a match to the semen found on Janey Carlton. You can't get better rock solid proof than that!"

Crane could see that Anderson was becoming as agitated as he was. They were both fed up of bungling around in the dark, making progress with the case, and then suddenly having their evidence shot to pieces.

"Look," Crane said, "I'll ring Billy and get him to talk to the adoption people and the Catholic Home again while we're in with Mrs Carlton. Perhaps by the time we come out he'll have something for us."

Anderson nodded and Crane made his call.

Sitting down in front of Mrs Carlton, they found she had pulled herself together somewhat, but Crane knew they would have to tread carefully as her emotional state was clearly very fragile, so Anderson was going to take the lead on this one. It was felt Crane's military boots weren't as subtle as the policeman's shoes.

"Mrs Carlton," Anderson said. "Thank you so much for waiting. What can you tell us about Janey's twins?"

Mrs Carlton beamed, "She said they were ever so lovely, looked like two peas in a pod. They let her hold them for a few minutes before they were... they were..." Mrs Carlton gulped back her emotions, "taken from her."

"So soon after their birth?" Crane had to speak, he was so shocked.

Mrs Carlton nodded. "It was standard practice back then. If the babies were being adopted, they were taken from the mother straight after birth, so they wouldn't have time to bond with her, or some such reason." Mrs Carlton wiped away her tears. "Barbaric, that's what I call it. I remember when Janey was born and I can't bear to think what it must have been like for her to have her babies ripped from her arms and carried off. Screaming and crying she said they were."

"Did they tell her where they were going? Who they were being taken to?"

"Not really. All they said was that they had already found parents for Tyler and that they were sure it wouldn't take long for them to place Zane."

"Tyler?"

"Yes. That was what she called them, Tyler and Zane. She specifically asked if they could keep those names. Oh, sorry, I already told you that, didn't I last time we met."

"Well you told us about Zane," grumbled Anderson and Crane wondered where the detective's empathy had gone. "It seems you'd forgotten about Tyler."

Mrs Carlton turned red and fell silent. Then seeming to gather her courage, she sat up straighter in the chair and said, "I hadn't forgotten about him. It was bad enough that Janey had one child at her age. I wanted to save her the shame by telling you she had two. I didn't think it would matter. One or two, what difference would it make? But after reading the papers, where it said that you were close to making an arrest…"

"You wanted to make sure we had all the information, not half of it." Anderson still seemed unimpressed by her late confession.

Mrs Carlton nodded, her eyes filling with tears.

Crane said, "Thank you, Mrs Carlton, you've been most helpful and if you remember anything else in the future that could be useful …"

Mrs Carlton took the hint, "Of course, Mr Crane. I'll let you and Mr Anderson here know straight away."

She grabbed her handbag off the table and went to the door and Anderson sent a passing policeman to escort her out of the building.

"Very nicely done, Derek," Crane rolled his eyes, "Very empathetic."

"Alright, don't rub it in. It was just that I felt so cross. I watched her, sitting there like butter wouldn't melt in her mouth, as though she hadn't done anything wrong and then crying! For goodness sake."

"She's lost a lot, Derek," Crane said. "Her husband is dead and her daughter murdered. Now we're dragging up memories of her two lost grandchildren. It would be a bit too much for anyone to have to deal with, let alone a woman in her 70's."

"Oh I suppose so," Anderson said as they walked out of the door and along the corridor in the direction of Anderson's office. "Get on the phone to Billy, see if he's had any luck with the Catholic home yet and I'll phone the lab about the DNA."

But as it turned out nothing had changed. Billy had received the cold shoulder treatment yet again from the adoption authorities and the Catholic home and all the lab said was that the sample from Tyler definitely matched the sample taken from Janey Cunningham. Crane put his head in his hands. They really were getting nowhere.

Forty Nine

Whilst Taggs Island might look beautiful, serene and peaceful on a sunny day, it looked pretty much like anywhere else in the grey drizzle that cloaked the Thames that morning; drizzle that was doing a good job of getting Saunders well and truly wet. It wasn't raining exactly, but the droplets of mist had soaked his hair and water kept dripping irritatingly into his eyes.

Brushing the moisture away, yet again, he knocked at the next houseboat on his list. The details of all the owners of the houseboats that Jeff Buckley had given to him yesterday hadn't revealed much. There was no one by the name of Zane anybody and no Tyler Wells either. It could be that Zane was using yet another alias that they weren't yet aware of, or that he wasn't tied to the island at all. Sagging under the weight of his depression, Saunders knocked at the door of a one storey houseboat, smaller and less conspicuous than most of its neighbours. But Saunders could see right away that there was nobody at home. The windows were shuttered closed, there were no plants or furniture on the deck and it had an air of abandonment about it. The paint was peeling in places on the wooden cladding and the bottom of the door had been kicked open that many times that the previous colour paint was bleeding through. Saunders knocked anyway.

His knuckles rapped against the door. Silence. Listening carefully for any sounds from the inside, all he could hear was the lapping of the water and the dripping of the drizzle from the trees. Here and there he could hear the voices of the rest of the team who were going around the island interviewing the residents. So far no one had recognised their picture of Tyler Wells. Giving up, Saunders crunched along the gravel path out of the small garden and round to the next boat.

It seemed he might have more luck this time. The windows of the houseboat blazed with light, he could hear a radio playing quietly inside accompanied by the sound of washing up. His knock was answered by a rather attractive woman who Saunders put at mid-60's. Her make-up was subtle and her short white hair softly framed her face. She was wiping her hands on a tea-towel.

"Ah, so it's my turn is it, officer?" she grinned.

"Your turn?"

He immediately felt stupid when she replied, "It doesn't take a genius to work out that the police are walking around the island interviewing everyone."

"No, sorry."

"Is it about the bodies?"

She wasn't the first owner that had asked him that, the rumour mill was obviously alive and well on Taggs Island.

"Sorry ma'am I can't comment on that. Are you," Saunders checked his list, "Judith Moulton?"

"Yes, that's me. I've been here for over 10 years

now. When my husband died I bought the boat as I wanted to be close to London but still be in a community. Best thing I ever did."

"I'm sure," murmured Saunders, realising she could be crossed off his list. "Have you ever seen this man on the island?" He held out his photograph without much hope of getting a positive answer.

She took it and stepped backwards into the light. Saunders hoped he might be invited in for a cuppa, but no such luck. Instead she said, "Yes. He's my neighbour that side," and she pointed to the empty boat Saunders had just been to.

Saunders consulted his list. "Would that be Mr and Mrs Jackson?"

"Oh no, they're in Dubai for a few years, so they rent out their houseboat occasionally. This photo is of Tim Bench."

"Any idea what he does, this Tim Bench?" Saunders struggled to keep the excitement out of his voice and remain impassive.

"Oh, he says he's a writer and he travels a lot for his research, so he's not here most of the time. Probably comes a couple of times a month for a few days at a time."

Scribbling furiously in his notebook, trying not to tear the damp pages, Saunders said, "Mrs Moulton, would you mind if I came in and asked you a few more questions?"

Taking in his sopping clothes she said, "If you take your shoes and wet coat off and dump them over there," she pointed by the side of the doorway, "I'll go and make us a cup of tea. One sugar or two?"

Saunders could have kissed her.

Fifty

Instead of going to arrest Tyler, Crane and Anderson reluctantly set up an interview with him and his solicitor. Not quite the impact they had hoped to make. When they met, Tyler Wells was clearly unnerved by the request and sat on the purposefully uncomfortable plastic chair, tapping his heel on the floor, next to his solicitor. Charles Walker sat back and studied Crane and Anderson with something akin to amusement as they walked in through the door and settled themselves at the bare wooden table. Crane hated the man as much as he had the first time they'd met, when Walker had successfully bulldozed his way through their case and managed to get Tyler released on bail. Crane wanted to wipe the self-satisfied smug off the man's face.

"Thank you for coming," said Anderson to the two men, with a politeness that Crane found galling. "We've asked you to come in as there is some new evidence we'd like to discuss with you."

Charles Walker put a restraining hand on his client's arm, as Tyler seemed about to speak, and asked Anderson to explain.

"We've had a visit from Mrs Carlton." At Tyler's

puzzled expression, he continued, "Janey Cunningham's mother, your maternal grandmother."

Tyler reeled back at the news, his mouth opening and closing like a guppy. But before he could say anything, Walker once again stopped him and motioned for Anderson to carry on speaking.

"She has informed us that Janey Carlton gave birth to twin boys and had specifically requested that they be named Tyler and Zane. They were taken away from her moments after their birth and given up for adoption."

"They?" asked Tyler. "You mean my brother and I? I have a twin brother?"

"That's correct," said Crane watching Wells closely, who clearly had no idea of his background. The look of astonishment on his face was akin to the gape of an unprepared lottery winner.

"You mean I have a living grandmother? A real biological grandmother? I'm not sure I ever wanted to know all of this," Wells shook his head and then shook his solicitor's hand away. "Let me speak," he said turning to Walker, "This needs to be said." Turning back to Anderson and Crane he blurted, "I was happy in my life, felt comfortable, secure, in control. And now? Now I feel like I'm losing my mind! I feel I'm being disloyal to my adoptive parents, who have never been anything but wonderful to me, so understanding and so kind. And this is how I repay them, by getting arrested for murder and for my birth family to invade my life as though it were their right. They have no rights. Those rights were given up when my mother gave me away. I don't want any of this."

"Please, Mr Wells," said Anderson.

Tyler Wells stood and said, "Don't please me. You bastards are ruining my life. I'm in danger of losing everything. My wife, my family, my job and my home and I haven't done anything. Not a bloody thing!"

As Charles Walker calmed his client and cajoled him into sitting down again, Crane fancied that really the bloke needed to talk to a counsellor, not shout at a couple of policemen who were only doing their job when they'd arrested him for murder. And nor was Tyler off the hook. His DNA was still a match to the semen found on Janey Carlton, so they could still prosecute. Wells was only on bail, not declared innocent because of the latest revelations. A fact Charles Walker would no doubt make sure his client fully understood.

"For the moment you will remain on police bail," said Anderson. "But we need to ask that you please contact us if your brother Zane gets in touch."

"Do you think he will?" asked Walker, eyes wide, horrified by the thought.

"It's a real possibility. Now we know that Zane does exist, and that your client's reports of someone in his house and his credit card details being stolen could in fact be true, it stands to reason he might well want to take things further. Instead of stalking Tyler, he might now want to meet him."

"Why? Why should I?" shouted Tyler. "Why should I help you lot?"

"Because you'll be helping yourself as well don't forget," said Crane. "You'll need him if you want to prove that he killed his mother and not you."

"I don't want anything to do with him." Tyler folded his arms and Crane thought the man looked like a sulky teenager.

"But…" said Anderson.

"Don't but me," spat Tyler. "How can I even speak to someone who killed his mother? Who had sex with his mother before he killed her! It makes my skin crawl."

"Possibly had," interjected Crane, just for the hell of it.

"Definitely had," retorted Tyler, "Because I bloody well didn't."

"I think we need to leave it there, for now," said the solicitor smoothly. "Thank you for the information, Inspector, Sgt Major. You'll be in touch if you hear anything else?"

"You can count on it, sir," said Anderson and Crane watched the two men leave the room, the urbane solicitor and his crumpled client.

Fifty One

The day was not being kind to Tyler Wells. Two companies he'd invested in on behalf of clients were in free-fall and all he could do was to watch the red blinking lights that showed the decline in the price of their shares. Then a pitch he'd made to a potential new client had been turned down and the business given to a rival firm. He only hoped the day wouldn't get any worse. Glancing at his watch he saw it was 1.30, so he decided to go and grab a sandwich that he would eat at his desk. And a good cup of coffee wouldn't go amiss, a large one.

As Tyler was shrugging into his jacket, his phone rang. He was so desperate for the coffee that he could already smell its enticing aroma, but his work ethic kicked in and he answered the call, albeit none too happily.

"Hello, Tyler," a voice he didn't recognise said.

"Who is this?" Tyler stilled.

"Oh I forgot, we haven't actually spoken before have we?"

The smooth baritone washed over Tyler, who couldn't place the voice at all, but at the same time it was vaguely familiar. He sat down in his chair, unsure as to what to do.

"Who is this?" he repeated.

"Zane," the man replied.

The chill that ran through Tyler's body made him shudder. He looked around to see if anyone was watching, witnessing this unexpected phone call, but of course everyone was too caught up in their own work to bother with him. Tyler's skin started to tingle with fear.

After a couple of false starts Tyler managed to croak, "What do you want?"

"Ah, I hear from your voice that you know who I am. It's your long lost twin, who is lost no longer. I thought it was about time we met."

"Why on earth would I want to meet you?" Anger was rising in Tyler now and he inhaled sharply. "What could we possibly have to say to each other?"

"Oh I'm sure we'll find some common ground. I really would advise that you meet me, it would be in your best interest."

"Really?" Tyler's voice was increasing in volume and not wanting to be overheard he lowered it and hissed, "In my best interest? Why should I want to meet the man who is fucking up my life?"

"Maybe I should have said it would be in the best interests of your wife and children. They are beautiful by the way, those adorable twins of yours. And as for Penny...."

"Don't you dare speak of my family; they're nothing to do with you, with us, with this."

"As I was saying," the smooth, chilling voice of his twin continued, "I'm sure you wouldn't want anything to happen to that lovely wife of yours, with her long blond hair and long legs. Have you realised just how much she resembles our mother? And we both know what happened to her, don't we?"

Tyler stood, "Don't you dare touch my wife!"

"Then meet me and I won't."

Looking around, Tyler realised he was attracting attention. He smiled weakly at his colleagues and fell back down into his chair.

"Come on, Tyler, you know I can get into your house. You've seen how much I can mess with your life and believe me, I've only just started. So unless you want a leading role in your own worst nightmare, meet me at Taggs Island tomorrow at noon."

"Taggs Island?"

"Yes. I've a houseboat there. It's really a rather pretty place and I'd love for you to see it. It's so tranquil on the river. It might help your bad mood, sooth your anxieties, enable you to regain some balance in your life. Drive in over the bridge, I'm on 'Dragonfly'. Turn right at the end of the bridge and it's the fourth boat down. Don't be late, I'm preparing something special for lunch and I wouldn't want it spoiled."

"You sick fuck," Tyler spat into the phone, but Zane wasn't listening. He'd already disconnected the call.

Fifty Two

Making like they were visiting a friend for coffee, Saunders and Crane were dressed down and sitting in the salon of The Falcon (as they'd been told that was the proper name for a living room on a houseboat) with cups of coffee in their hands and chatting in a desultory way to Jeff Buckley and Judith Moulton. Crane looked at his watch, just one more time he promised himself, and found it was still only half past eleven. Exactly the same time as it had been when he'd last checked it. There were thirty minutes to go before Zane and Tyler met.

Saunders hadn't been able to find Zane or Tim Bench as he was known on Taggs Island, so their only way of catching him was by gate crashing the meeting between Zane and his brother Tyler. Hence the mock up coffee morning and hence Penny Moulton being kept away from her own houseboat that was berthed next to 'Dragonfly', Zane's houseboat.

Both Jeff and Penny had agreed to help the police, but Crane got the impression that it was only to protect Taggs Island and its houseboat owners. Saunders had asked the neighbours on either side of the houseboat, to ring him if the tenant was seen on the 'Dragonfly' but he wasn't sure that they would have done. Crane agreed with the policeman, that the island was all a bit too private and introspective for him. Taggs Island residents seem to protect their own, shutting out the outside world, happily cocooned in their own bubble. All seemed to be artists, writers, photographers and musicians and all were more interested in their art than what was happening around them. Even now Buckley and Moulton were talking about improvements to the island that were under discussion by the Residents Association and how in future maybe they should stop owners from renting out their properties. For wasn't this an example of having undesirables in their midst?

Crane stood, shaking out his khaki coloured trousers and pulling down his polo shirt. One look at his image in the glass wall only confirmed his suspicion that he still looked like a soldier. Glancing over at Saunders, he was relieved to find that the policeman also looked stiff and uncomfortable in the jeans and sweatshirt that he was wearing instead of his suit, but maybe it was the wait that was getting to him.

Crane opened the patio doors and stepped onto the deck of the Falcon. Nothing much was stirring, only a couple of ducks gliding along past the boat. They nudged up to the hull as though they were hoping for a few bits of bread, but when none were forthcoming from Crane, they lost interest in him and swam away. Crane could see the bridge that linked the island to the shore from his vantage point but was glad that he couldn't see the back-up team of policemen who were waiting, hidden in the foliage, ready to grab Zane if he got away. Downstream, Crane knew the Marine Police Unit launch was also waiting, to intercept Zane if he tried to get away by water. Crane looked at the river again, hoping none of them would end up in there, for it looked particularly grey and uninviting, not to mention bloody cold.

Crane couldn't sense any movement from Dragonfly, nor could he hear the sound of feet on deck. The sense of anticipation was building in Crane, so much so that he could taste victory. His teeth were on edge as though he was in the dentist's waiting room and his tongue had a metallic taste to it. They were so close now. Surely their prey couldn't get away? For if he did give them the slip, Crane was convinced Zane would reinvent himself once more and they'd never find him.

He'd wondered why on earth Zane had called Tyler in the first place, but Saunders had said that it was classic psychopathic behaviour. Zane wanted validation for his crimes. He needed to boast of his prowess to the man who would appreciate it most of all; his twin brother. He must see his twin as an extension of himself and needed to brag of his achievements, wanting and needing his brother's validation.

"More coffee, Tom?" came the call from Buckley, and so Crane left the deck to return to the salon. Best to keep things looking as normal as possible.

Fifty Three

Tyler had never felt more intimidated than he did now. The thought of meeting his brother, his sick, twisted brother, made Tyler's stomach clench. He'd already been to the toilet on the way there, but still his body was insisting on physically manifesting his fear. He'd been in tense situations before, of course he had, but they were all to do with work. The last time he could remember being so nervous was when he'd asked Penny to marry him. Oh, and waiting for her at the altar, that was pretty scary as well. But those were good pains of anticipation. He hadn't been filled with feelings of dread then, as he was now.

DI Anderson was in the car with him and running through all the possible scenarios he might encounter. But Tyler couldn't keep his mind on the policeman's words, as images of Penny kept skittering them away, as if they were nothing more than bowling pins being crashed out of existence by a ball. Then, memories of his girls intruded, and Tyler had to suddenly stop the car. Barrelling out of it, he ran to the hedgerow at the side of the road and folding in two, leaned over the grass and heaved. But all that came up from his stomach was bitter bile, making him feel worse than he had before. Once he had calmed down enough to straighten, he saw Anderson holding out a bottle of water.

"Here," Anderson said, "try some of this."

Tyler sipped the water gratefully, but not before he'd noticed his hands trembling as he tried to get the bottle to his lips.

"I always find thinking of something else works, when I'm in a tense situation," said Anderson.

"That's what I just did. I thought of my wife and kids and then, without warning, had a vision of what Zane could do to them," Tyler shuddered. "I'm not sure I can go through with this."

"I do understand, Tyler," Anderson said. "But believe me it will be in all our interests to get Zane. As you just said, it doesn't bear thinking about what he could do if left unchecked."

Tyler couldn't stop the moan escaping from his lips and wanted to throw up again.

"Do it for your family, Tyler," pressed Anderson. "Come on, you're a hard-nosed businessman aren't you?"

Tyler replied, "Yes," even though he wasn't sure Anderson had meant it as a question.

"Well then, if ever you needed to be that man, now is the time. Treat this as a business deal, a meeting with an awkward client, try and step outside of your emotions."

Tyler turned and looked at the policeman, who he knew was only trying to help him.

"Look, Sgt Major Crane has to do that all the time," Anderson said. "He once explained to me that a soldier has to compartmentalise, separate army from family.

When at work, they have to give the job their full attention, follow orders, react to situations, fall back on their training and then when at home, well, all thoughts of work need to be banished and the focus shifted to the family. That's what you have to do now. Just see this as a job. Nothing to do with Penny and the kids. For now they don't exist. All that matters is this meeting with Zane and catching the bastard. Can you do that?"

Tyler thought back to how life was before Zane, before all this nonsense, this upset, this chaos. Going to work every morning he would slough off the family and their wants and needs and focus on being a hedge fund manager, giving that his full attention until it was time to return to being a family man. He guessed that was what Anderson wanted him to do. So he looked the policeman in the eye and nodded. He'd try his bloody best at any rate.

"That's great, Tyler," Anderson said and put a comforting hand on his shoulder. "Right, we better get going. It's five minutes to twelve and you've got to drop me off before you reach the bridge."

Fifty Four

Dropping Anderson off at the pre-arranged point, Tyler called the policeman's mobile and they made sure they were both connected. It had been decided not to bug Tyler, as no doubt Zane would find it, or have jamming equipment. They had to remember he was a sophisticated hacker and computer expert. So they were relying on old fashioned technology and hoped to at least be able to hear and record part of their conversation.

Tyler nosed his car over the bridge, following Zane's directions. He stopped outside Dragonfly and sat for a moment looking around. The boat's windows were open, but not the door. The garden needed some attention, as did the boat. Both had an air of neglect and Tyler found this at odds with Zane's supposed urbane, sophisticated, polished persona that Anderson had described.

As Tyler climbed out of the car and walked towards the houseboat, he heard his every footfall as though magnified through a megaphone. He was walking slowly, wading through an invisible force field that was tugging at his arms and legs, as he struggled to get to the door. He raised his hand to knock on what he assumed to be the front door, but it opened before his knuckles could make contact with the wood. As the door swung open, there was no one there. Tyler sent up a quick arrow prayer, asking God for his protection, before he stepped onto the boat.

"At last," said a voice behind Tyler.

Tyler swung round and stared… at himself. His eyes widened in horror and he stumbled backwards and closed his eyes in a vain attempt to rid his brain of what he'd just seen. His twin really was identical, even down to the slight dimple in the chin and the way his hair fell on the crown of his head. The only variation between them was the clothes that Zane was wearing. The apparition that was his brother was eyeing Tyler with amusement.

"Bit of a shock isn't it, coming face to face with yourself. That's just how I felt when I saw you."

Tyler felt the boat move under his feet and his head swam, so he tottered over to a sofa and collapsed into it.

Ignoring Tyler's distress Zane said, "I hope you're hungry, brother dear," and he walked through to the open plan kitchen. He lifted up a lobster that was trying feebly to grab at its captor with claws that were taped together. Tyler glanced at the hob, where a pan of water sat merrily bubbling. Tyler nearly threw up and fumbling in his pocket, grabbed a handkerchief that he held to his mouth.

"Interesting creatures, lobsters, don't you think?" Zane chatted, seemingly oblivious to Tyler's horror. "Like most arthropods, lobsters must moult in order to grow, which leaves them vulnerable. During the moulting process, several species change colour. But they soon grow hard shells again and are ready to continue their life along the sea bottom. But changed, of course, as they become bigger and stronger we each moult."

Tyler could relate that analogy to Zane, as was no doubted expected of him. But Tyler likened him to a chameleon as well, able to change his colours to suit whatever each occasion expected of him.

"Put your phone where I can see it," Zane said.

Tyler grabbed his phone and while his hand was in his pocket, he managed to end the open call to Anderson, before putting the mobile on the small table. He was aware the policeman hadn't got much any evidence from the conversation, but at least the police now had confirmation that Zane was on the houseboat.

To Tyler's revulsion, Zane held the lobster over the boiling pan of water, ready to drop it in, but then appeared to change his mind and put it back on the counter.

"So, how does it feel to be meeting your twin brother in the flesh?" he asked. "Can't you feel that already there is a connection between us? It's like sharp volts of electricity coursing through our bodies."

Tyler managed to gabble, "What do you think you're doing? What's going on?"

Zane laughed, but there was no mirth in it. "Nothing's going on. Why shouldn't I want to meet my brother?"

"What about the sick things you've been doing?" Tyler wanted to stand and confront his brother, but was sure his weak legs wouldn't hold him and wobbling or falling down wouldn't help the impression that he was trying to give, that he wasn't frightened of Zane. But he was. Very. So he stayed seated.

"Sick things? What are you talking about?"

"Killing Janey Carlton, our mother. Oh and don't forget the fact that you had sex with her first."

Zane roared with laughter. "Oh that's a good one, Tyler, and just how do you know it was me?"

"Because they matched your DNA to samples left on the body."

"You mean your DNA, don't you?" Zane stared at his brother. "We are twins after all," Zane's pupils had become dark pin prinks that he focused on Tyler.

Hearing a noise outside, Tyler and Zane both looked out of the window of the houseboat, over the river, towards the bridge connecting the island to the bank of the Thames. Policemen could be seen moving along it. Police cars were forming a barricade at both ends of the bridge, which probably meant they were already moving through the island towards the boat

"So you've been helping the police," Zane said. "I should have known. But know this, Tyler, because of your treachery, because you have turned in your brother, your only brother, I will bury you under an Armageddon of bad luck. Your life will be constantly disrupted. I can get your bank accounts closed, your credit taken away, have loans taken out in your name that aren't repaid, oh and don't forget the photos of your lovely Penny that I've got and can splurge all over the internet. What would the girls think of their mother when she has half naked, provocative pictures, out on the World Wide Web for all to ogle?"

As he was speaking Zane was moving towards the front door. Standing to the side of it, he opened it a crack. Tyler stood, but still couldn't see what Zane could through the open door, but assumed it must have been a policeman, as Zane closed the door and ran across the room. Tyler stepped forward to stop him, but Zane pushed him out of the way causing him to fall to the floor hitting his head on the coffee table on the way down. He saw Zane disappear through the patio doors before everything went dark and the world receded.

Fifty Five

Crane and Saunders were still on Jeff Buckley's boat from where they'd been keeping a surreptitious eye on the river and on the island, but they hadn't seen Zane from their vantage point. Crane's phone buzzed in his pocket, signifying a message and he opened it to find it was from Anderson. At last, confirmation that Zane was on the boat with Tyler. The wait was over.

Thanking Jeff for his time and help, and ordering him and Judith to stay on the boat until the police came to let them know it was safe to leave, Crane and Saunders made their way round to Dragonfly. Creeping through the garden, they arrived at the front door. Crane heard the lapping of the Thames against the houseboat, the rustle of the grass as something slithered through it and murmured voices from inside. As Crane and Saunders both heard the footsteps from inside the boat coming in their direction, they flattened themselves against the side of the boat, positioned on either side of the door. Unseen by Zane, who opened the door a crack and then closed it, Saunders and Crane then each made their way along the opposite sides of the boat, moving around to the length of houseboat that faced the river. As Crane emerged from his side of the houseboat, he saw Zane clambering into a small boat with an outboard motor. As the motor spluttered into life, Zane began to edge the boat away from the side of the houseboat.

Afterwards, Crane couldn't have said what made him do it.

He wasn't aware of any conscious thought, never mind making a cognisant decision, he just gave himself over to his training. His reactions kicked in and he jumped, pushing himself off from the deck of the houseboat and reaching for the small vessel drawing away from him, as though he were a swimmer reacting to the buzzer signifying the start of a race. There was no way the bastard was going to get away from Crane. If they lost him now, they might never find him again. As Crane belly flopped into the water, arms outstretched, he managed to grab the side of the boat, pulling it down into the water with him. Then he dragged himself through the river and managed to kneel on the rim of the boat, forcing it further downwards into the water, tipping the other side of the boat upward. Looking up, he saw Zane teetering on the sloping bottom of the boat, a look of pure hatred on his face, before Zane tumbled past him and joined him in the water.

Letting go of the boat, Crane allowed himself to be drawn under the water, hoping to see Zane. But all he could see was murk and weeds. The water was too cloudy to see the bottom of the river. Closing his eyes against the dirty water, which was causing his eyes to sting, he pushed up and broke through the water, taking deep lungsful of air. As he turned to look around, Zane's head bobbed up right next to him. Pulling his arm back and punching Zane as hard as he could on the jaw, Crane managed to disorientate Zane enough to grab the man's clothing from behind and begin swimming towards the houseboat in the classic lifesaving position, towards Saunders' reaching arms.

Passing his inert bundle to Saunders, Crane grabbed the side of the houseboat and allowed himself to relax. Hanging there, legs floating behind him he watched as several uniformed policemen crashed through the patio doors onto the deck of the houseboat and helped Saunders pull Zane out of the water. They laid him face down on the deck and handcuffed his hands behind his back.

Once they'd done that Crane called out, "Hey, any chance of a boost up?"

Several pairs of willing hands grabbed at Crane's hands and clothes and pulled him clear of the water and he tumbled over the side of the houseboat to join Zane on the decking. After catching his breath, he looked up to find Saunders grinning down at him.

"Didn't know you were such a good diver, Crane," Saunders called. "That was worthy of first prize in a belly flopping contest."

"Fuck off," said Crane, standing and grinning as he dripped water onto the deck, squelching along in his waterlogged clothes. "Anyone got any dry clothes I could change into?"

Looking down at his soggy trousers and polo shirt, Crane was glad that he hadn't ruined one of his work suits and as he started shivering, he acknowledged that he had been right on one point at least. The water was bloody cold.

Fifty Six

The paramedics from the ambulance the Metropolitan Police had brought with them, ministered to both twins. Zane was treated for the after effects of the river and swallowing large amounts of disgusting murky water. He was also given a tetanus jab as a precaution, as Crane had split the skin on Zane's jaw when he hit him with a right hook.

Tyler was treated for shock, after his encounter with what he kept calling that evil, sick, bastard and for the large bump on his head from his collision with the table. Every time he saw his twin, Tyler began shivering with fear, shouting to Crane and Anderson that he never should have agreed to meet Zane. He should have listened to his solicitor and kept well away from their stupid sting operation.

Anderson was trying to mollify Tyler yet again, when Crane gratefully took the hot drinks that he'd cadged off Jeff Buckley. After handing one each to Tyler and Anderson he put his head round the ambulance door and said, "Oh, sorry, Zane, I forgot to get you a drink," and stood there sipping his own coffee and observing the twin, who was also shivering, but from cold, not from fear. The paramedics had stripped off Zane's clothes and wrapped him in a blanket and some sort of foil covering, reminding Crane of the thermal sheets handed out to runners after the London Marathon.

Zane's face was grey, from his dunking in the water and the cold, but there was no mistaking the zealous fire burning in his eyes. "You fucking bastards," said Zane. "You'll pay for this."

"Don't think so, Zane," said Crane and he looked pointedly at the handcuffs binding Zane to the metal frame of bed he was sitting on.

Zane rattled the handcuffs. "These won't hold me for long," he sneered. "My solicitor will soon have me released."

"I wouldn't be too sure about that," said Crane, sitting on the steps of the ambulance. He really could have done with a cigarette to go with his coffee, but they'd been in his pocket when he went into the Thames and he couldn't believe it when he found out that no one else on the team smoked. So caffeine would have to try and do the job of the absent nicotine. "DC Saunders wants to talk to you about the death of your mother. Oh, and let's not forget about the four bodies he found in the river, downstream from your houseboat."

"You'll not find a shred of evidence to prove that I have ever killed anyone."

"Maybe, maybe not, but there's lots of evidence proving that you put the fear of God into your poor brother over there."

"Ha," laughed Zane. "That idiot? Look at him. He's a wreck, a basket case. Who's going to believe a word he says?"

Crane had to acknowledge that Tyler Wells was

indeed a blubbering mess at the moment, but Crane was sure he'd find some backbone from somewhere and hoped very much that DC Saunders could find some evidence proving that Zane had stolen Tyler's identity.

"Anyway," continued Zane. "How are you going to prove which one of us killed our mother? We're identical twins remember?"

Crane looked into Zane's eyes again. This time they weren't sparking with anger, but boring into Crane with an equal, but this time, ice cold intensity. Crane had seen looks like that before. They didn't frighten him, just hardened his resolve to bring the bastards to justice. As for the DNA evidence, well he'll just have to see what else the forensic laboratory could come up with once the houseboat has been examined and all the evidence collected.

"Well, it was nice to chat to you," said Crane standing up and draining the last of his coffee. "Time I was off. You coming?" Then he laughed. "Oh no, I forgot, you're the criminal. You can't just get off that bed and go home. All you have to look forward to is a small cell at the police station and then another one in a local prison. On the other hand, I'm off home to be with my family. Enjoy!"

Fifty Seven

But Crane wasn't feeling quite so cocky the next morning when he met Anderson at Aldershot Police Station. Feeling far more comfortable, as he was once more dressed in his usual uniform of black suit and white shirt, he stood in Anderson's office and said, "Are you sure?"

"Positive. The houseboat is clean. Professionally cleaned, in fact. The only prints there are Zane and Tyler's from yesterday and those were lifted from the kitchen and the living room or whatever they call it."

"Salon."

"Sorry?"

"On a boat it's called a salon."

"Oh, well," huffed Anderson. "As I was saying before you rudely interrupted me, not only was the houseboat clean, but so was the laptop that was left there. We interviewed the residents who were in yesterday, yet again, and they all parroted Zane's cover story of him being a writer and not there very often. No one had seen him arrive with any girls, or dump any of them in the river. But there's no writing on the laptop, no book, no articles, no internet history, nothing."

"Bugger," said Crane sitting down and waving away the offer of a cake. "How are the interviews going?"

"As you would expect, Tyler Wells is blaming Zane and Zane is blaming Tyler. Clearly the boat isn't Zane' primary residence, but we can't find any records of any other address, at least not under that name."

"What name?"

"Oh, right, sorry you don't know. He's calling himself Zane Zwicky now, not Tim Bench."

"I beg your pardon?"

"I know, ridiculous isn't it? He says the name Tim Bench is a pen name. Fucking prick. It's as though he's taunting us. There is a flat registered in the name of Zane Zwicky in Crouch End and Saunders has a crew going through that now, but he told me he doesn't hold out much hope. It seems it's just like a dead drop address, part of his cover story of being a writer."

"Shit."

Crane had been hoping that today would be a good day. He'd been sure they'd find lots of evidence tying Zane to the killings and to his infiltration of his brother's life. But it appeared not. They'd hit yet another brick wall. They were stumped again, confronted with yet more lies and deception.

As Crane went through every scenario in his mind that he could think of, to get at the truth, Anderson's phone rang and Crane was vaguely aware of Anderson answering it and carrying on a conversation. Crane stood intending to go outside for a cigarette, but then Anderson started frantically gesticulating. It seemed he wanted Crane to sit back down again.

Anderson clattered down the telephone receiver and said, "That was DC Saunders."

"I take it there's news. Either that or you're jiggling

up and down because you need the toilet."

"Funny," said Anderson clearly thinking the remark was anything but. "One of the pathologists from the investigation into the dead girls in the river has called. He's found something. Skin under the nails of one of them. It was buried deep under the side of the nail which is why it wasn't washed away by the water and it's a match to the DNA found on Janey Carlton's body."

"Gotcha," said Crane.

"Yes, but which twin is it? They've both got the same DNA."

Fifty Eight

It had taken some doing, but eventually the Metropolitan Police had been persuaded to do further tests on the DNA taken from Tyler and Zane and that taken from Janey Carlton and from the poor, as yet still unidentified, dead girl from the river. Anderson had explained to Crane that there was a laboratory in Germany that could do further testing on the samples, this time going through the entire DNA strand. In standard DNA tests only a tiny fraction of the code is analysed - enough to differentiate between two average people, but not identical twins. In a test case, the German laboratory had taken samples from a pair of male twins and looked at the entire three-billion-letter sequence, and they'd found a few dozen differences in their DNA. Having analysed the results, they were confident that they could now tell one twin from another. The Met had taken advice from the Department of Public Prosecutions who had agreed that if the testing revealed differences in the DNA of Tyler and Zane and then those differences could be matched successfully to the DNA found on Janey Carlton, then they could confidently proceed with a prosecution on that basis.

The problem was what to do with the twins during the month that it would take to get the results? Which was the reason Crane and Anderson were sat in the back of a courtroom in London, waiting for Tyler and Zane to be brought in to appear in front of a local Magistrate. Their respective solicitors were pressing for bail while the testing went on, which was fair enough.

Saunders slipped in next to Crane as the Magistrates entered the courtroom and the case against Tyler Wells was heard. The DPP lawyer argued for remand in custody, but Tyler's solicitor emphasised that Tyler was not a flight risk. All Tyler wanted to do was to go home and be with his family and there was no way he'd leave them. He'd proven that time and again, especially as he'd helped the police catch his twin brother. After a few minutes consultation with his two fellow magistrates, it was agreed that Tyler would be granted bail, but his passport had to be handed in and he would have to wear an electronic tag. Tyler was taken back down to the cells, crying with gratitude, to await finalisation of the paperwork.

Then it was the turn of Zane. He was dressed in a sober suit, looked in complete control of himself and his emotions, unlike his twin, but he also managed to appear contrite, keeping his eyes down, sitting perfectly still, awaiting his fate. Crane frowned at him in dislike and disgust. Then the whole palaver started again. The Magistrates heard the pleas from both sides and came to the same conclusion. Zane could also be released on bail under the same conditions. They'd allowed it for one twin and felt it was only right that the other should be treated the same, as they were both charged with the same offence.

Crane was flabbergasted and barged through the courtroom doors and out into the hallway.

"What the hell was that?" he rounded on Saunders. "How can they possibly let that piece of shit out on bail?"

"I assume you're talking about Zane," said Saunders.

"What? Yes. He seems by far the most likely candidate for the murder."

"I totally agree."

"So how come you lot let him walk?"

Saunders grinned. "Just go and wait outside, Crane. I'm sure you need a cigarette by now."

Crane scowled again, but followed Anderson out into the open air. After pacing around and smoking two cigarettes he eventually said to Anderson, "Look, I don't know what the hell we're waiting for. Can't we be off now?"

"This. This is what we're waiting for," said Anderson and pointed to Zane as he emerged from the courthouse, grinning and talking animatedly to his solicitor.

As the two men walked down the stone steps, Saunders approached them from one side and two uniformed policemen from the other. Coming to a halt in front of Zane, Saunders said, "Zane Zwicky I am arresting you on suspicion of the murder of Clarice Walton. You don't have to say anything..."

As Saunders' read Zane his rights, Crane looked as bewildered as the accused himself. "What the fuck?" he hissed at Anderson. "How the hell did Saunders manage that?"

"Thought you'd enjoy Saunders' little spectacle, Crane," Anderson said. "The mystery girl in the river, the one with the DNA under her nail, has been identified as Clarice Walton. The Met had deliberately kept quiet about her, treating her murder as a separate case, so they could re-arrest Zane, just in case he was granted bail today."

Crane grinned, "Which he was."

"Yes, just as we thought. And now instead of going home, he'll be going back to prison."

"What if he gets bail again for this offence?"

"Saunders and his bosses are sure that no magistrate will bail him when he's charged with the murder of four girls. They're confident he will be held for the month it will take for the DNA results to come through. Not a bad plan, eh?"

"A right result, Derek, that's what it is. A right result."

Fifty Nine

Anderson was ready. Well, as ready as he'd ever be. His stomach was fluttering, his palms sweaty and he kept moving, putting his weight first on one foot and then the other, just as though it were mid-winter, not a beautiful, surprisingly warm, spring morning. He was sweating slightly, dressed as he was in his beige raincoat, which he'd come to consider his lucky raincoat. So, just as a precaution, he was wearing it in the hope that nothing would go wrong. He daren't take it off and jinx the operation.

Stood on the edge of Hampstead Heath, Anderson's gaze kept being drawn to the view. The Heath, one of the highest points in London, was a sprawling area of heathland and parkland, offering a range of leisure activities and, of course, the famed panoramic view of the city of London. But he wasn't there to admire the view. He was there as the team assembled, before their foray into Highgate Village.

Saunders walked up to him, a broad grin on his face, "Ready, Derek?"

"Been ready for the past hour," Anderson replied.

"I know, still, we're a go in," Saunders checked his

watch, "five minutes. The spotters have confirmed he's in-situ and the armed response officers are assembled and ready."

"Do you think there's going to be trouble then?"

"It never hurts to be prepared, especially not with a collar as important as this."

Derek nodded his agreement. The police preparations had been on-going over the past day and night. Everyone in the team had been made to bunk down at the training establishment where the plans were drawn up and finalised. No one was allowed to go home, or call home, not until it was all over. They'd left at 5 am that morning, in order to be in place by 7 am.

*

Crane checked his watch for the umpteenth time that morning. He'd left the training establishment with the others at 5am and was now sat in a car with a colleague of DC Saunders, who wasn't very chatty. In fact the man hadn't said a word since Crane had parked up 30 minutes ago. All Crane knew about him was that his name was Tony.

Looking out of the car window, wistfully wishing for a cigarette that he couldn't have, Crane watched the street in the early morning light. In past times Crane imagined a milkman would be clanking up and down the street at this time of day, his bottles rattling as he ran from door to door. These days no one used a milk man anymore, preferring to buy their milk at supermarkets which were open 24 hours a day and where the prices were as cheap as chips and the milk treated for longer-than-ever-life.

He mused on the twins living so close to each other

and wondered if it had been a deliberate act on Zane's part. One living in Hampstead Village and the other in Highgate Village. One twin fully aware of where his sibling lived. The other happily oblivious.

Crane mused on the differences between the two men. Could it really be a different upbringing that had wrought the changes between them? Or were the differences the lab had found in the DNA strands responsible for one turning out to be a model citizen and the other a psychopathic killer. It was all above his intellectual grade, but an interesting question to ponder for all that.

At precisely 7 am Crane's radio crackled into life.

*

Captain Draper was sat in his car, outside the imposing Georgian house in Farnham, dressed in uniform, as he was on official business. His task was to tell Major Cunningham the outcome of the Met's investigations and the news that the killer had just been arrested. It had been agreed that everything would be done at the same time as a precaution against a leak, either to the criminal, or to the press. That the twin about to be arrested could get wind of what was going on, was too awful a scenario to contemplate. More than that, it would make the army look like a bunch of numpties. Not that it would have been a fair allegation, of course, but when were the press ever fair? When did they ever worry about the truth? Their number one priority was selling newspapers. They were not concerned with the probability that what they printed, under the guise of news, was capable of ruining people's lives.

The Major was still suspended and Draper wondered

what would happen to the man's career now. Even though the case was about to be brought to a successful conclusion and the Major had been cleared of any involvement in his wife's death, he still couldn't see how the Major could continue in the army. Everyone now knew about his private life. There was nowhere left to hide. It would probably be best for him to quietly retire. Either that or he'd face being tied to an inconspicuous desk job. No soldier wanted that, Draper certainly wouldn't.

Looking at his watch, the minute hand clicked over to the top of the hour. 7 am. He'd get a call on his mobile any minute now.

*

Highgate Village was quiet as Anderson followed behind the team who would be going in first. They were armed with automatic rifles and handguns, and their beloved battering ram. As the men ran for the house, police cars drew up at either end of the road, blocking possible escape routes. With an almighty crash the front door was battered in, splinters of wood flying at the heads of men, but falling harmlessly to the floor after hitting the plastic visors of their helmets.

Voices could be heard calling out, "Armed Police! Come out with your hands up!" over and over again, interspersed with, "Clear," as each room was searched and then sealed off. Anderson and Saunders stepped past the broken door as the voices continued to assail their ears. The calling was meant to disorientate the man they were after and as far as Anderson was concerned it was doing a good job. The voices echoed through the large house and boots could be heard thundering up the stairs.

Then Saunders' radio crackled into life. "Found him. Suspect has been neutralised and secured. Stand down. I repeat, stand down. Mission accomplished."

Anderson and Saunders exchanged broad grins as the prisoner was escorted down the stairs and brought to a standstill in front of them.

*

Crane's mobile buzzed with a message. "All went well, suspect in custody and en-route to New Scotland Yard."

Crane allowed himself a grin, before nudging Tony and saying, "We're on."

The two men left the car and walked across to the Victorian terraced house. Crane opened the gate and walked along the original paving and rapped on the stained glass set into the front door. Crane didn't like having what he thought of as a 'minder'. Tony followed him around like a shadow, but Saunders had insisted. The twin deserved the courtesy of a visit from the Met as well as from one of the original investigating officers, so Crane kept trying not to think of Tony's presence as a babysitter.

The man who answered the door had clearly just got out of bed. His hair was dishevelled, his chest bare. He wore a pair of cotton pyjama bottoms and his bare feet were poking out from underneath them.

"Sorry to bother you so early in the morning, sir," said Crane, as a look reminiscent of a startled deer caught in car headlights passed over the man's face.

"You!" he managed to say. "What? Why?"

"Could we come in for a moment please, sir," said

Crane and walked through the door uninvited as the astonished man stood aside.

*

Captain Draper got the same message from Anderson at 7.05 am and walked along the deserted driveway to the front door. All was quiet. There were no lights on inside that he could see, no noise of a television or radio. Ringing the doorbell in three long bursts, Draper then stood back from the step and waited.

Footsteps could be heard pounding down the stairs and a rather out of breath Major Cunningham threw open the door. He looked puzzled to find Captain Draper standing there. Frowning he glanced around to see if anyone else was with him and then he seemed to recover as he barked, "What the hell do you think you're doing, Draper? Why are you ringing my doorbell at this time in the morning?"

Jesus wept, thought Draper, the bloody man never changes, the autocratic and authoritarian bastard. Swallowing his anger Draper said, "I wanted to come and personally give you the good news, Major. Perhaps we could go inside?"

"Good news?"

"Yes, sir, good news."

"Oh, well, you better come in."

As the Major closed the door behind them, he said, "Come into the kitchen, I've just made coffee. I expect you could do with one as well?"

"That would be very kind, sir, thank you."

The kitchen was all bleached wood and marble tops, gleaming in the spotlights set underneath the wall cupboards. A distressed table and six chairs sat on the other side of an island and Cunningham placed two cups of coffee on it. Sitting down, Captain Draper said, "I'm here to tell you, sir, that a suspect has just been arrested and charged with the murder of your wife. The Metropolitan Police have taken him into custody and he's at this very moment on his way to New Scotland Yard."

Major Cunningham closed his eyes and exhaled loudly, nodding his head to himself, as if to say, thank God, it's really over now.

"Who was it?" asked the Major in a voice that was little more than a whisper.

Sixty

DI Anderson and DC Saunders stood in the viewing room, watching the prisoner being interviewed by the chief investigating officer of the team that worked on Janey Cunningham's murder, of which Saunders had been a vital part.

"You don't mind that you're not doing the interview then?" asked Anderson.

Saunders shook his head. "Nah, I got to go with the arresting team. That was good enough for me."

"It's been a hairy 24 hours though," said Derek. "I couldn't believe it when you rang with the news yesterday that he'd been released on bail."

"It came as a shock to us all, I can tell you. The boss nearly had a heart attack. Thank God the laboratory in Germany were ready to release their results. We needed their DNA analysis to make an arrest. An arrest and charge that would stick this time."

"And thank God for the fact that the police detail who followed him from the courtroom yesterday didn't lose him."

"Mmm," agreed Saunders. "Especially when he went to an address in Highgate that we knew nothing about.

He was ready to ship out, you know. We found packed suitcases in the bedroom and in the room he used as an office. I suspect we'll find details of an airline booking in due course."

Anderson laughed, "No doubt he was going to a country that doesn't have an extradition treaty with the UK."

"The only place he'll be going now is prison, from where he'll never leave. Not with multiple counts of murder on his record," said Saunders.

The two men fell silent and listened to the voices coming through the speakers.

"On what basis are you arresting my client?" they heard the man's solicitor ask. "What possible evidence could you have to tie my client to these murders? It looks to me like you've got the wrong twin."

The CIO smiled, obviously relishing his moment. After a small pause he slid a report across the table.

"This report confirms that the DNA found on the bodies of Janey Cunningham and Clarice Walton matches exactly the DNA sample given by your client Zane Carlton." The solicitor went to interrupt, but the CIO held up his hand to stop him. "The DNA samples underwent extensive testing and 10 points of difference were identified between Zane here and his twin Tyler Wells. Therefore we have irrefutable evidence that Zane Carlton killed the two women."

Turning his attention away from the on-going interview, Derek said to Saunders, "What about the other three girls? Any chance of justice for them?"

"Well, it doesn't look as though we've any evidence to tie him to those murders, so whilst we're convinced he killed them, we can't arrest him for them."

"So it's a case of two out of five isn't bad?"

"Something like that, Derek, but he won't be seeing anything of the outside world until the day he dies and he'll only leave prison in his coffin. So at least they'll get poetic justice. Which is better than no justice at all."

Sixty One

…Zane had been left alone at last. He looked around the impersonal space of the police cell. Plastic coated walls, a CCTV camera in the corner, a moulded plastic bed and a door. Not much to hold his attention. He swung his feet off the floor and laid down on the hard surface, linking his hands behind his head. It looked like all he would have to look forward to for the rest of his life was reliving his memories. Who'd have thought the scientists could come up with a way to make such a detailed analysis of DNA? And who'd have thought the police would pay up for it?

Still, he'd had a good run. He smiled to himself at the thought of his encounters at the Mayfair Club. He also smiled at the memory of his cat and mouse games with Tyler. But at the thought of his twin brother, Zane's good thoughts threatened to fly right out of his head, to be replaced by the dark envy he harboured against his brother.

But the one person he hated above all others, of course, was his mother.

Things had been going so well with her. He'd been happy to pay for her services, he earned enough and the experience was worth every penny. Nothing needed to change, but she'd had other ideas.

That last afternoon she'd told him it was to be their last encounter. When he'd pressed her for information, she'd told him she no longer needed to earn money that way. He'd been about to congratulate her on getting more modelling work, but the words had died on his lips when she'd confessed to having fallen in love. She was leaving the Major, modelling and her sexual exploits and running away with the new man in her life. Her face had lit up at the thought of her new gigolo and her eyes had shone as they'd never done for him.

That's was when, for the first time in his life, he'd begged. Begged her to go away with him instead, for wasn't he the one who worshiped and adored her? Wasn't he the one who couldn't bear to be apart from her and had found her again after that pig of her husband had kept her from him. He should be the love of her life, he, Zane, no one else. If he couldn't have her, then no one else would either.

He'd moved quickly and put her hands through the loops of plastic already placed on the bed posts. One of their favourite sexual games was to have Janey tied up, lying underneath him, helpless, ready to be ravished. Once she was in his power he'd said, "You can't leave me. Don't you realise who I really am?"

She'd shaken her head in confusion. But when he'd told her he was her long lost son, instead of arching her body to receive him, she'd begun to struggle.

His hands had found their way to her throat as she'd taunted him. "Get off me you filthy bastard, you're no son of mine, how could you be? Screwing your mother? What sort of sick, twisted individual are you?"

"I'm what you made me, you bitch," he said, slapping her face. "You left me. Abandoned me."

"It's a good thing I did if this is what you've turned out to be...."

Those were the last words she'd ever spoken. His hands had tightened around her neck until she was unconscious, but she couldn't be allowed to die straight away. He'd yet to take his revenge. He'd ripped a lamp from the side of the bed and begun to beat her body with it. Her perfect skin split and bled, bruises appeared on her arms, torso and legs and then, with one final cry, he smashed the lamp into her head.

Spent, he'd climbed off her inert body. After he'd untied her hands and feet, he wiped down the apartment as best he could using cleaning fluid and a cloth he'd found in the kitchen.

With one last look at what he'd thought was her dead body he'd walked out.

Sixty Two

The cold lager slid down Crane's throat and he put down his glass with a sigh of appreciation and wiped his mouth with the back of his hand.

"Thanks, Derek, did I ever need that."

Anderson smiled, "I think we all did."

"So, now you've told us about the arrest of Zane," Draper turned from Anderson to Crane, "how did it go with Tyler Wells?"

Crane glanced around the pub before speaking. There was the usual early evening crowd in the Goose, most of them strung out around the long bar. He, Anderson and Draper were sat towards the back of the large room. No one was sitting near them, which was why they'd chosen that table, for privacy.

Crane said, "He led us into the kitchen, confused and to be honest more than a little frightened by our visit, which you'd expect. Once I explained about the results of the extended DNA testing and confirmed that we'd arrested and charged Zane, he just crumpled. He'd been leaning against the wall and he literally slid down it, put his arms around his knees and sobbed with relief."

"He'd been under tremendous pressure," said Draper. "Everyone had doubted him for months. Does he have any plans for the future?"

"Well, just then, Penny came into the kitchen and after she'd comforted her husband and helped him into a chair, she said that as it was all over they'd be moving."

"Where are they going?"

"She said anywhere that isn't obsessed with the case. But they thought that somewhere like the Lake District sounded good. It would take some while before Tyler was recovered enough to get a job, after his mental breakdown following the confrontation with his brother, and the constant publicity and intrusive presence of the press wasn't helping him. They're desperate for a fresh start."

"What about the Major?" Anderson asked Draper.

"When he'd finished blustering and shouting at me for long enough to hear me out, I got pretty much the same emotional reaction as Crane did. He sagged against the table, put his head in his hands and sobbed."

"What do you think will become of him?"

"I think his army career is finished. His father was telling me that they're talking about Clive going back home and learning how to run the family estate from his brother. They've been talking about it apparently and Quentin has some good ideas about increasing the production of the farmland and his father was thinking about opening the house to the public. To be honest, I think that's for the best, the Major's reputation within the army is too tarnished. I don't think he'd ever recover from the scandal, as least not as far as the army are concerned."

"This case has wreaked havoc on all their lives,"

Crane mused. "Families have been decimated. Mrs Carlton has lost her daughter and found her twin grandsons, only to find out that one of them is a serial killer and the other doesn't want anything to do with her. Major Cunningham has lost his wife and ruined his career and Tyler Wells has been scarred for life, even though he was found to be innocent."

"People never fail to astound me," said Anderson. "Even after all my years on the force it seems I can still be surprised. The ramifications of this case are pretty damn wide reaching. Families ruined, an army career ruined, a career in the City ruined and five women dead."

"It just shows," said Crane, "how the vagaries of the human psyche can come back to haunt you. A mistake over 30 years ago, ended up with Janey losing her life and ruining the lives of countless others." He fell silent.

"Jesus Christ," said Draper. "I think we're getting too maudlin here. We're supposed to be celebrating the successful conclusion of the case, not getting depressed by people who seem to have no control over their impulses. So," he said draining his beer glass and holding it up. "Anyone want another?"

Past Judgment
Author Note

Her Majesty's Young Offenders Institute (HMYOI) in Reading is no longer a working institute. However, the building is still there and plans are being considered by Reading Council to turn it into a hotel and leisure complex.

The prison has a long and rich history and its most notable prisoner was Oscar Wilde, who wrote the Ballad of Reading Goal, based on his incarceration there.

I worked as a teacher in the Education Department at Reading HMYOI, teaching a range of subjects including English, Maths, Computer Skills, Art and, rather badly, Cookery. I loved my time at Reading and also at other nearby prisons, where I did supply teaching. My family has experience in prison education. My father was Deputy Chief Education Officer for Prisons and Borstals in England and Wales in the 1970's and 1980's and my mother taught at Reading Prison and Broadmoor. Both had the dubious pleasure of meeting some of Britain's most notorious prisoners.

Whilst the Judgment series may draw on our experiences from time to time, all characters and events are fictitious. Although I try and be true to policies and procedures, this is a work of fiction. Therefore, all mistakes are my own.

About Past Judgment

The past has a way of catching up with you....

At least it does for Emma Harrison, newly appointed assistant governor for inmate welfare at Reading Young Offender's Institute and for Leroy Carter, a prisoner who has been convicted of murder. When the prison van taking Leroy to Dartmoor crashes and he escapes, he's hell-bent on proving his innocence.

Leroy and the original detectives on his case, have to face the past head on. But so does Emma, when a fellow passenger from the train hijack three years earlier walks back into her life.

Can Leroy prove his innocence? And has Emma exorcised the ghosts from her past?

1
Present day...

The prison transport vehicle Leroy was expected to climb into loomed into view. It was very large and very white and would carry him away from Reading Young Offenders Institute. From the security of all things known. His well practiced and comfortable routine. His cell mate, John. His courses in the Education Block. And, of course, Emma. Or rather Miss Harrison. He shrank back. Fearful. Unwilling to get into the claustrophobic cell he would be locked in. He turned slightly as if to run away, but the prison escort officer he was handcuffed to wasn't having any of it.

"Come on, lad. Leroy isn't it? In you go, it's not that bad when you get in there."

Leroy had to disagree with that one and wondered if the escort had ever had to travel in one of those 'cells' for any length of time.

"But..."

"No buts, in you go," and Leroy took one last deep breath of fresh air before he and his three travelling companions were pushed and pulled into the vehicle as though they were no more than cattle being herded into a milking shed or an abattoir. As Leroy climbed the two steps into the transport, he was told to stop opposite the second cubicle on his left. When he was told to get in it, Leroy looked at the escort then at the cubicle and wondered how the hell he was supposed to do that. There was very little room in the narrow space to even turn around. Especially for someone as tall and gangly as he was. Standing at over six foot, but without the bulk and muscle to make him intimidating, Leroy had taken to stooping over slightly. A posture that screamed leave me alone, I'm trying to make myself small so as not to be noticed.

"Back in, then I'll close the door and you can hold out your hands through the space in the bars," the exasperated officer told him. "Then I'll un-cuff you and you can turn and sit down."

Leroy managed to do as he was told as the door was banged shut. Then locked. Breathing deeply to try and stop the rush of claustrophobia from his brain flooding through his body, he looked out of the window. Glad for the small glimpse of the world outside. Focusing on the window, he tried to block out the noises of the back door being slammed and locked and then the cab doors being opened and closed. As the rumble of the diesel engine started its soundtrack to their journey, the van left Reading HMYOI, rumbling along the urban roads on its way to the motorway.

As they started their creaky, bumpy journey, Leroy's fellow prisoners made their feelings known. At the top of their voices. From abuse hurled at the escort officers and each other, to sexual references tossed in the direction of any woman unlucky enough to be passing by. They seemed to have an opinion on everything and everyone. Leroy added an extra layer on top of his claustrophobia. Fear. He was straight out scared of his fellow travellers. He hoped this noise and abuse wasn't a sign of things to come at Dartmoor Prison. So far the whole experience wasn't a good start to his new life in a new prison. He shrunk away from the noise, trying to blot it out, pushing back into the seat and turning slightly, trying to keep his back to the other prisoners.

Once on the motorway, the gentle rumble of tyres on asphalt calmed Leroy and he was able to relax a little and inspect his surroundings. Not that it took very long. He was sat on a grey plastic seat in a space smaller than an old fashioned telephone box. But a Dr Who Tardis this wasn't. The space wasn't larger inside than it seemed on the outside. White plastic was everywhere, gouged with irreverent messages from previous occupants. There was nothing to read, nothing to occupy his mind and he sunk into a daze. He became drowsy and must have dozed off, for he was woken by a dramatic clap of thunder.

The view outside his aircraft-type window was obscured by dark heavy clouds. They looked full of the rain they seemed determined to dump on the road. He watched with mounting fascination as the big fat heavy rain drops began to fall. One, two, four, eight, sixteen... until they fell so fast Leroy couldn't count them anymore. The drops fell faster and harder, bouncing ankle high off the ground, their rapid tattoo drilling into his brain. A tattoo that became louder as the raindrops turned into hailstones, some as large as golf balls. They carpeted the road, turning it into a white, icy, highway to hell.

The van, unable to find purchase on the road, began to veer first one way and then the other and Leroy, with nothing to hold onto, put his arms out and placed his hands palm up on each wall. Wet with sweat, they simply slid off the plastic. As the van swerved, Leroy went with it, unable to do anything but ride the storm. He heard tyres squeal as the van slewed sideways. With a bang, the van hit an unseen object and fell over, sliding along the road as though it were still on its wheels, not on its side. Leroy was thrown out of his seat and ended up lying, face down on the side wall that had suddenly become the floor.

After several seconds of screeching metal grinding against the road and Leroy feeling like he was on fairground ride, the transport ground to a halt. For a moment all was still. The kind of pregnant pause found inside the eye of a tornado. The brief period of calm, before the world descended into chaos once again. The other prisoners all began shouting at once. Cursing the weather, the officers and the van. But underneath their yells Leroy could hear something else. He tuned out the yelling from his fellow prisoners as best he could, concentrating on the underlying sound. He recognised it as water. Water that was gushing and gurgling. That's when Leroy realised the van must have fallen into a river. His fears were confirmed when he felt his trousers getting wet. Water was permeating the prison van, seeking out and finding the smallest of gaps. Unchecked. Leroy and his fellow prisoners couldn't get away. The cubicles, so small and narrow, meant they were unable to stand. The doors were locked so they were unable to escape. There was no sign of the escorts. And the water was rising.

You can purchase Past Judgment at Amazon.

Meet the Author

I do hope you've enjoyed Solid Proof. If so, perhaps you would be kind enough to post a review on Amazon. Reviews really do make all the difference to authors and it is great to get feedback from you, the reader.

If this is the first of my novels you've read, you may be interested in the other Sgt Major Crane books, following Tom Crane and DI Anderson as they take on the worst crimes committed in and around Aldershot Garrison. At the time of writing there are seight Sgt Major Crane crime thrillers. In order, they are: Steps to Heaven, 40 Days 40 Nights, Honour Bound, Cordon of Lies, Regenerate, Hijack, Glass Cutter and this one, Solid Proof.

Past Judgment is the first in a new series. It is a spin-off from the Sgt Major Crane novels and features Emma Harrison from Hijack and Sgt Billy Williams of the Special Investigations Branch of the Royal Military Police. At the time of writing the second book, Mortal Judgment has just been released. Look out for more adventures from Billy and Emma in the Judgment series in the near future.

All my books are available on Amazon.

You can keep in touch through my website http://www.wendycartmell.webs.com. I'm also on Twitter @wendycartmell.

Printed in Great Britain
by Amazon